PUFFIN B

THE A–Z ~~DJINN~~ DET

If Parinita Shetty ever met a djinni who offered to grant her three wishes, she would be that maddening sort of person whose first wish would be to ask for more wishes. She accidentally wrote her first book, called *The Monster Hunters*, in 2013. *When Santa Went Missing*, her second book, was published by Puffin Books in 2014. Her second wish would be the ability to teleport to any corner of the world. Her third wish would involve chocolate cake.

ALSO IN PUFFIN BY PARINITA SHETTY

When Santa Went Missing

The A-Z Djinn Detective Agency

Parinita Shetty

PUFFIN BOOKS

An imprint of Penguin Random House

PUFFIN BOOKS

USA | Canada | UK | Ireland | Australia
New Zealand | India | South Africa | China

Puffin Books is part of the Penguin Random House group of companies
whose addresses can be found at global.penguinrandomhouse.com

Published by Penguin Random House India Pvt. Ltd
7th Floor, Infinity Tower C, DLF Cyber City,
Gurgaon 122 002, Haryana, India

First published in Puffin Books by Penguin Random House India 2017

10 9 8 7 6 5 4 3 2

ISBN 9780143334552

Typeset in Crimson Text by Manipal Digital Systems, Manipal

Printed at Repro India Limited

www.penguin.co.in

PROLOGUE

The python slowly coiled itself around the young man's body, its scales rippling in the moonlight.

The man's eyes widened. He found his left arm pinned to his side; he couldn't move it, no matter how hard he tried. He wriggled violently in an attempt to get the snake to stop squeezing him. That only goaded the python into tightening its grip around his chest.

The man used his free arm to grab the python's tail and began unravelling the snake. When it realized what was going on, the python stiffened, using its sheer strength to become as hard as slithering steel.

The man sighed in frustration and managed to unearth a hip flask from his right pocket. He used his mouth to open the bottle, spat out the lid and poured the alcohol over the python's head. The liquor flowed into the snake's open mouth, causing it to retch and loosen its grip.

'You are throwing a tantrum,' the man addressed the python. 'This is not how you resolve conflicts.'

In response, the python stiffened around the man, then disappeared, to be replaced by a thick, foul-smelling fog that enveloped the man's head. The man wrinkled his nose in disgust and broke into a fit of coughing, before tightening his fingers around the book in his left hand.

'I am not changing my mind,' the man gasped, clutching at his throat. He was finding it difficult to breathe.

The stench grew stronger. The man fell to his knees and began wheezing violently. Just as it seemed like the man was going to faint, the fog vanished and a menacing creeper started to grow up his legs. The plant twisted around both his ankles as it inched its way up to the arm. The man grabbed the plant with his right hand and held the book above his head.

'You are being immature,' the man admonished the plant. 'Wanting to tell people about another world is not a bad thing. It is *your* world. You should be pleased. Instead you are trying to strangle me!'

'I am only trying to strangle you because your plan is dangerously idiotic,' the plant replied.

The man unwound the creeper from his body and shook it off on to the floor. The plant remained motionless for a moment, before transforming itself into another young man, lying sprawled on the ground. He brushed the dust off his trousers as he stood up, pointed a finger at the first man and froze him to the spot. He then sauntered over and plucked the book from his grasp.

'THAT DOES NOT BELONG TO YOU!' the immobilized man bellowed. 'GET BACK HERE, DJINNI!'

The djinni walked away, stopped near a pile of dry leaves and flicked his fingers to set the leaves on fire. He lazily held the book over the smoking heap, waiting for the flames to grow.

'NO!' The first man broke out of the spell's grasp and ran headlong into the other figure. The djinni tumbled face first into the fire. The flames suddenly turned into a mound of pillows, cushioning the fall of both man and djinni. The two of them lay on their backs, breathless.

'What . . . is . . . *wrong* . . . with you?' the man panted.

'That is why we have gone out of fashion,' the djinni replied. 'Humans have become too sensitive to some light-hearted violence.'

'Give it back to me,' the man demanded.

'Not until I see what you are about to do.' The djinni rolled over and grabbed the book, which had skidded away during their fall.

The book was covered in purple leather, with its name stamped in bright gold letters. The djinni skimmed through the pages and began to laugh.

'What?' the man snapped.

'*This* is your plan?' the djinni chuckled. 'I had no reason to be worried after all.'

'I don't know what you mean,' the man said icily. 'I let that book go out into the world, and a fortunate person discovers Djinnestan.'

'Anybody who reads this ridiculous tome is sure to think it a fairy story,' the djinni snorted. 'Most humans do not believe in Djinnestan any more, remember? Most humans do not deserve to.'

'That's where this comes in.' The man reached into his pocket and took out a piece of paper. The djinni snatched the sheet and examined it carefully.

'A summoning spell?' He finally eyed the human pityingly.

'It's the one I used to get you here,' the man said, miffed at the djinni's condescending tone.

'And what if it falls in the hands of one of those dangerous humans?' the djinni inquired innocently. 'You seem to find them everywhere these days.'

'He'll think it's a fairy story, I presume,' the man replied coldly.

'You went through a lot of unnecessary trouble with the summoning,' the djinni pointed out. 'Half these things are preposterous.'

He bent down to pick up a twig. As he straightened up, the twig turned into a pen. The djinni began to write furiously on the piece of paper he was holding. The man stood silent. When the djinni was done, he thrust the sheet into the man's hand and smirked.

'So you've decided to help, but be mean-spirited about it, I see,' the man observed.

'My curiosity has been sparked, that is all,' the djinni shrugged. 'When the next person to summon a djinni uses it to destroy the world, I assume your face is going to be quite amusing to behold.'

'What's the Museum of Unusual Objects?' Ashwin asked, twisting around in his chair to look at his mother.

Mrs Kamath was supposed to be dressed for work, but under her crisply ironed black shirt, she was wearing pyjama bottoms with purple cows drooling all over her legs. Her hair looked like a mischief of mice had partied in it the previous night, and her left cheek wore a streak of flour. Ashwin wondered what would happen if she were suddenly teleported to her office looking like that.

She looked away from the eggs scrambling on the stove and glanced distractedly at her son. 'What? the Museum of—'

'It's number ten on The Summer List.' Ashwin pointed at the refrigerator.

Mrs Kamath collected fridge magnets, and the top half of the refrigerator was full of magnets her friends had brought back from all over the world. Four of the magnets held recipes, two held Ashwin's drawings of

Sherlock Holmes and the Famous Five, and the one shaped like a Japanese geisha held a long sheet of paper. The Summer List, as Ashwin called it, was something his mother had come up with. The title of the list announced:

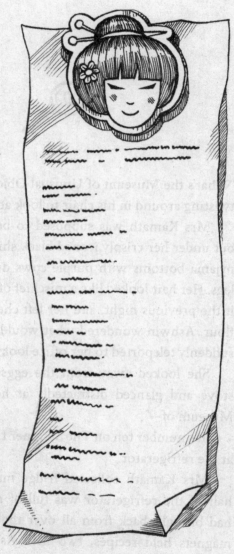

Things for Ashwin to do in the summer vacation so that the TV doesn't turn his brain into soup

The two of them had already checked a few things off the list.

1) ~~Explore the caves on Elephanta Island~~
2) Go on a nature trail at Sanjay Gandhi National Park
3) Attend the children's film festival at the National Centre for the Performing Arts
4) ~~Go for a play at Prithvi Theatre~~
5) Build the Hogwarts castle and its grounds on the beach
6) Discover the universe at the Nehru Science Centre and Planetarium
7) ~~Go on a tree walk in the Maharashtra Nature Park~~
8) ~~Draw superhero/supervillain pictures of the sea creatures at the Taraporewala Aquarium~~
9) Look for clues during the scavenger hunt in Bandra
10) Go to the Museum of Unusual Objects

Ashwin was intrigued by the tenth entry on the list. It sounded deliciously mysterious.

'Oh, that. Yeah, I'd read an article about it a few weeks ago.' Mrs Kamath went back to making breakfast. 'It's run by a rich old lady who loves collecting strange things. Somebody suggested that others might like to see her collection, so she's opening her house to curious people.'

'A museum in a house!' Ashwin exclaimed. He couldn't imagine fitting a museum in his own tiny flat. Their new apartment was the latest in a long series of houses he and his mother had to shift into over the years. Ashwin had been very excited about this one because, for the first time

3

in his life, he had his very own bedroom—it used to be a balcony and was barely bigger than the bathroom, but it was his favourite space in the house.

'How cool! What kind of strange things does she have, Mom? Do you think she has an alien in the museum? Or a piece broken off a spaceship? Maybe she has stones which turn metal into gold. Or maybe she has a mummy!'

'A mummy isn't strange,' Mrs Kamath replied. She was now spooning the eggs on to two plates. 'You saw one at the Egypt exhibit in the museum last year. Do you want jam or Nutella on your toast?'

'But this mummy has two heads,' Ashwin said matter-of-factly. 'That would be a pretty unusual object, right? Nutella, please!'

'Definitely.' Mrs Kamath laughed as she spread some chocolate on two slices of toast and ruffled her son's hair affectionately.

'Mom!' Ashwin moaned. 'You got Nutella in my hair!' He tried to rub his wild curls clean, then wiped the chocolate on his Iron Man T-shirt when his mother wasn't looking.

'We can't go to the museum this week, though,' he reminded her through a mouthful of eggs. 'We're going book shopping this Sunday, right?'

'We'll have to,' Mrs Kamath nodded. 'You've finished all the books you picked up two weeks ago. So what are you going to do today?'

'It's a secret,' Ashwin retorted, taking a bite of the toast. 'I'll tell you when you get home tonight. You've bought the lemons, right?'

'They're in the fridge,' his mother replied. 'Though what you're going to do with so many lemons, I have no idea!'

'You'll see,' he said mysteriously, shooting her his biggest Cheshire-cat grin.

Ashwin had a summer list of his own:

How to Earn Money and Make Friends
by Ashwin Kamath

Class Five was going on an educational field trip to Gujarat just before the summer vacation ended and the new academic year began. And Ashwin desperately wanted to go on the trip with his class because he was convinced that it would be his last chance to make friends.

When he had transferred to Akshara High School in the middle of last year, Ashwin had found that everybody in his class already had their own groups and best friends. Even the new building he and his mother had shifted into, which was one of twelve buildings in a quiet housing society, only had children who were either too young or too old to play with him.

Ashwin was so bored of having nobody to hang out with that he'd decided he was going to go on the trip and make a friend, no matter what. The only problem—there was no way he could actually go on the trip. Not on his mother's salary anyway. Ashwin knew that Mrs Kamath worked really hard in her office from Monday to Friday (and half the day on two Saturdays of the month), but she wouldn't be able to afford the Rs 7500 he needed to pay for the trip.

Ashwin's secret plan was to find a way to earn the money himself. After all, he had two months—*eight whole weeks*—he could use. He had even asked his teacher for special permission to pay the field-trip fee later than the rest of his classmates.

Unfortunately for him, three of the eight weeks had already passed and he wasn't much closer to his goal.

His first idea had been a huge disaster. He had spent a week collecting trash he could recycle, and another week making all sorts of objects—both useful and decorative—out of them. His mom had helped him with ideas. She'd looked things up on the Internet while he went through a craft book he had borrowed from his school library and forgotten to return. And then he'd held a sale in his housing society—just the previous weekend, in fact. He had put up posters advertising his sale and expectantly set up two tables full of his art in one of the society's hallways.

All the adults who saw him were very impressed. Half of them were so inspired by his project that they went home and made recycled art of their own. The other half thought it was the perfect way to get rid of some of the clutter at home and donated all their trash to his cause. The only grown-up who ended up buying anything from him turned out to be his own mother.

Ashwin was so disgusted by the adults in his housing society that he marched all his creations and their donations over to the local *raddiwala* and sold them for Rs 375. At least the raddiwala appreciated his art. One of Ashwin's art projects—the colourful ice-cream-stick-and-paper-boat mobile—hung proudly at the entrance of his tiny shop.

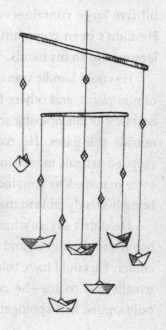

But having spent a weekend being hot and thirsty had given him the idea for his next fundraising project.

~~1) Recycled art sale~~
2) Nimbu-paani stall

The last straw was when the lady tried to call child protective services to take Ashwin into custody.

Ashwin could handle making enough nimbu paani to fill five large containers and all the bottles in his house. He didn't even complain about what squeezing all those lemons did to his hands.

He could handle transporting all those containers full of nimbu paani, and others full of ice, all the way to the front entrance of his housing society so he could set up shop just outside the gates. He didn't mind spending some of his recycled-art-sale money to buy four dozen plastic glasses, and even managed to convince the security guard to help him bring his study table to the gates to arrange all his things on.

He didn't say anything when the few people who did buy from him sighed and wished the nimbu paani had been colder. He could have told them what the hot summer sun usually did to ice—he couldn't control science!—but he only smiled half apologetically.

He didn't mind when a man running a sandwich stall in the next lane looked at his tiny nimbu-paani table and decided to set up shop right beside him. Ashwin figured that a snack could only add to his beverage business.

He began getting a little worried when a sugar-cane-juice stall followed the sandwich man's example, quickly followed by a *gola wala* and an ice-cream cart. Those last three businesses were in direct competition with his own!

He began to get *really* worried when some of the people from his society started grumbling about all the hawkers at their gates. And when a couple of hours later the police came to clear the illegal stalls away, Ashwin began to feel more than a little afraid. After all, it was his tiny nimbu-paani table that had led to all the trouble.

But it was when one of the policewomen started talking to Ashwin about child-labour laws, and insisted that he would be protected by people who looked after children forced to work for a living, that he  decided he needed a grown-up. Ashwin abandoned his stall and ran to his neighbour's house. Madhur Uncle always kept an eye on him when his mother was at work and had told Ashwin to call him whenever he needed something.

Ashwin rang the doorbell to his house non-stop until a harried-looking Madhur Uncle answered the door.

'I need to talk to Mom!' Ashwin shouted.

Madhur Uncle raised his eyebrows inquiringly and then glanced behind Ashwin. The stout policewoman who had chased the runaway boy stood panting at the staircase, clutching a stitch at her side.

'Why don't you come inside and sit down?' He invited Ashwin and the policewoman in. 'Ashwin, you know where the phone is. I'll get you both a nice, cold glass of nimbu paani while you call your mother.'

'I know I don't want your brain to turn to soup, Ashwin,' Mrs Kamath sighed in exasperation when the two of them sat in the living room later that evening, 'but I almost wish you were one of those kids addicted to the television!'

It had taken some explaining to convince the policewoman that the nimbu-paani stall had been Ashwin's idea. Mrs Kamath had promised her that she didn't profit off her son's labour, and even took out his fourth-standard report card as proof of his academic prowess.

After the policewoman left, Mrs Kamath had collapsed on to the sofa and muttered a quick prayer of thanks.

'It *was* a good idea, though, right?' Ashwin looked at his mom uncertainly. 'It would have worked if all those other people hadn't messed it up!'

'It was a very good idea.' Mrs Kamath smiled and ruffled her son's hair. 'But tell me, Ashu, why are you so impatient to earn money? Are you saving up for something? You can always tell me, you know.'

'No, Mom,' Ashwin said hurriedly. He didn't want his mother to get upset. 'I just do it for fun. In all the books and cartoons, kids are always coming up with ideas to earn money during the summer!'

'If you're sure,' replied Mrs Kamath, shooting her son an anxious glance.

'I gave two free glasses of nimbu paani to Oz Chacha today.' Ashwin tried to change the subject. 'I think that made him less grumpy than usual. But only a little.'

Oz Chacha lived on the street right next to their housing society. Most of the adults Ashwin knew made faces when they saw the homeless old man sitting on the street and held their bags and purses tighter when they had to walk past him. But his mother always smiled at him kindly and often gave him food, old clothes and books. Unlike any other homeless person Ashwin had encountered, Oz Chacha loved to read.

'Good boy,' Mrs Kamath beamed. 'As a reward, you can pick up an extra mystery book on Sunday.'

'Yes!' Ashwin punched his fist in the air. 'But that's two flop ideas in a row.' His face fell. 'I've spent more money on the plastic glasses than I earned.'

'I'll buy two glasses of nimbu paani right away,' Mrs Kamath said. 'Anything to feel better in this awful weather.'

But Ashwin wasn't listening. 'Maybe I can turn our house into a museum of strange things, too.' He began to sound excited again. 'Then I can charge for tickets like the other museums do . . .'

'I don't think we have enough things for a museum, Ashu,' Mrs Kamath pointed out.

'Then I should start collecting straight away!' Ashwin said eagerly. 'We already have some things I can add. The pyramid paperweight made of fossils. The potato which looks like an elephant. All those weird dust objects we find under the sofa. The boy puppet which turns into a girl puppet when turned upside down. That nose statue. All those postcards you collect but never send—'

'Don't forget your brain, Ashu,' Mrs Kamath laughed. 'The most unusual object of all!'

'I see two Famous Fives, one Feluda, one 39 Clues, one *The Case of the Candy Bandit* and nothing that's not a mystery.' Mrs Kamath looked at her son sternly.

Ashwin and his mother were standing outside a hole-in-the-wall store called The Book Shop. The Book Shop sold all kinds of cheap, second-hand books and boasted of a large collection of titles for children. It also functioned as a library of sorts because it allowed people to sell their books back for half the price. Ashwin had already returned the books he'd picked the last time and was desperately trying to decide which ones he'd take home now.

'But, Mom!' Ashwin wailed. 'They're all too good to leave behind!'

'You know our deal.' Mrs Kamath was unmoved. 'I want one non-mystery for every mystery you've chosen. And no more than six books!'

Detective stories were the only kind of stories that mattered to Ashwin, and had it been up to him, those were the only ones he'd read. Unfortunately, his mother had other ideas. She was determined to expand, if not change, her son's taste in book genres.

'But you promised I could pick up an extra mystery,' Ashwin reminded her.

'Which makes it four mysteries and two others,' Mrs Kamath replied. 'So put one of those away and pick two books with NO detectives.'

Ashwin grumbled but knew when he was defeated. He looked at *Five Go to Mystery Moor* longingly before putting it back on the tottering pile of Enid Blytons on the table. After hunting among the mounds of books for five minutes, he emerged with a book of poetry called *This Book Makes No Sense.*

'This one sounds funny,' he said as he offered it to his mother. She nodded her approval.

After picking up and rejecting several other books for sounding far too boring, Ashwin's eyes fell on a bright purple cover, with the book's title embossed in golden cursive lettering: *Adventures among the Djinn.*

It wasn't the kind of book he would usually have chosen. But for some reason he couldn't quite explain, Ashwin paused, his hand hovering over the slim volume, before picking it up and handing it to his mother.

'No detectives in sight!' he declared.

Mrs Kamath raised her eyebrow. 'Interesting choice, Ashu.'

'I hope someone's kidnapped and has to be rescued by a detective djinni,' Ashwin muttered, but quietly enough so his mother wouldn't hear.

Back in his room, Ashwin took out his notebook, struck the nimbu-paani-stall idea off his How to Earn Money and Make Friends list and added point number three:

3) A museum of strange things

What else can I do? he wondered. He looked around his room for inspiration. His eyes fell on his recently acquired pile of books.

I wish I could solve a mystery and earn a reward too, Ashwin thought as he chewed on the end of his pencil. *Or find a treasure buried on an island. But Mumbai doesn't have any secret islands. And Mom didn't allow me to look when we were on Elephanta Island.*

With no new ideas to inspire him, Ashwin soon grew bored and shut his notebook with a thump. Heading out of his room, he accidentally knocked over the pile of books on the table as his hand reached for the door. They tumbled over, exposing the purple one at the bottom.

Do djinn ever have to worry about money? Ashwin wondered as he bent down to pick up *Adventures among the Djinn*. He decided to settle back on his bed and opened the book to a random page. 'Oh, I bet they could just magically summon gold coins or something. I wish I had a djinni to grant me three wishes.'

As if the book knew what he was thinking, the first paragraph on page thirty-two stated:

Djinn cannot perform genuine miracles, only illusions of miracles. In the old days, they often created a problem and then 'showed up' to fix it. One of their favourite tricks was to make it look like a person was sick with fake physical ailments and then turn up to heal them in exchange for something.

Ashwin stared. He flipped to another random page and read:

Djinn are very sensitive, get easily offended and are extremely vindictive by nature. As a rule, they hate helping humans. The only way one can get a djinni to grant his or her wish is by summoning one to the human world. The only way a djinni can get back to Djinnestan is by fulfilling the wish. On rare occasions, a djinni will bestow wishes without being summoned, if he or she has taken a liking to a particular human.

'What sort of book *is* this?' Ashwin exclaimed in astonishment. It appeared to be a fake supernatural textbook, introducing the world of djinn.

I should have just sneaked in the Famous Five while Mom wasn't looking, Ashwin thought, rolling his eyes.

He snapped the book shut in disgust and threw it across his bed. He hopped off and made his way to the scattered books on the table. He chose a book at random, then turned back to his bed. That's when he noticed the wrinkled piece of paper which had slipped out of the book he had been reading.

He snatched up the small sheet, crumpled it into a ball and was about to shoot it into his dustbin, when something made him pause. He smoothed the paper out on his bed carefully. The paper was yellowing with age, and temporarily turning it into a ball had done nothing to improve its state of collapse. It looked like it had been torn out of a book—but not the one it had fallen out of.

Someone had also scratched out some of the words and scribbled in the margins and around the sentences. At the top of the page, in large, old-fashioned letters, it said:

The Art of Summoning a Djinni

To summon a djinni, you will need the
following items:

1) ~~A silver~~ mirror
   This is used to reflect both worlds—
   the human world *and* the djinn world.

   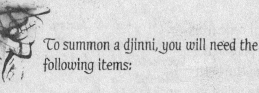

   (As if djinn care what your mirror is made of. They have more important things to worry about!)

2) Black ~~lipstick~~

   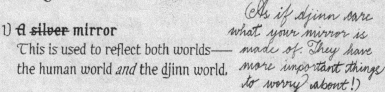

   (An oddly specific and completely unnecessary requirement. Anything black which will write easily on the mirror without permanently damaging it will work.)

3) ~~A~~ white candle, a red candle and a
   black candle
   The white and black candles represent
   the free will of the djinni, while the red
   candle, as well as the flame that will rest
   upon it, represents the fire which gave
   birth to the djinni.

4) ~~Incense~~

5) ~~Rose~~ water
   This is used to cleanse the room of any
   negative energy.

   (??? Good old filtered water works just as well.)

6) ~~Salt~~

   (Drawing things with salt is tricky and a waste of good salt. Use chalk instead.)

7) ~~An~~ item you wish the djinni to
   be bound to

This item must be a personal relic from your past. The stronger the personal meaning the item has for you, the better it will work. Many people use rings or pendants, since they are inconspicuous and easy to transport.

(All just a fancy way of saying — something which belongs to you that will not draw attention to itself, or you, if you choose to carry it around.)

The spell to summon a djinni must be performed on the night of a full moon, between midnight and 3 a.m.

First, find a quiet room to perform the spell in. While summoning a djinni, you must be completely alone.

(The time of day or month doesn't matter. Djinn like sleep just as much as humans do; don't wake them up at a ridiculous hour. And humans wonder why the djinn they summon are always so grumpy!)

Before you begin, light the incense and sprinkle rose water in the four corners of the room.

Use the salt to draw a circle around yourself and all the items you have collected.

Then use the salt to draw four small six-point stars outside the circle and one big six-point star inside the circle.

(You can make six-point stars by drawing two triangles cutting through each other.)

Set up the candles in a straight line on the floor in this order: white, red and black. Each candle should be about six inches away from the one beside it. *(No self-respecting djinni is going to measure the distance between candles!)*

To begin the spell, say the following words three times to open the gates between the two worlds:

Talizanza talizanza palizey nalipo

After you have said the spell, first light the white candle, then the black, and finally the red.

Use the black lipstick to write the following spell in the centre of the mirror:

Ackamarackus kemting teknaleb
Slartibartfast ahuru
Proverallyse leva rannygazoo
Fadoodle danistu

Then close your eyes, concentrate on the item
you are using to bind the djinni to, and say:

**I offer you this _____ as
your shelter in my world.**

To finish the spell, repeat the following
words three times:

Talizanza talizanza palizey nalipo

Then blow out the red candle, then the
black, and finally the white.

The spell is now complete. The djinni is
bound to you until they finish the task you set.

**Warning: Summon a djinni at your own
risk. Most djinn delight in spreading
mischief and mayhem and they love to
trick humans. Cast this spell only if
you know how to control a djinni.** (Utter nonsense, of
course. Djinn are
just like humans —
some good, some bad,
but mostly in-between.)

Ashwin read the instructions three times before carefully putting the page back inside the book.

'This *has* to be a prank,' he decided. 'Someone's playing a silly joke on me. Very funny, person who is trying to trick me into believing this. I'm not falling for it. Except . . . who would play a prank on me? I don't even know anybody here!'

As this realization slowly dawned on him, Ashwin's thoughts stopped short. On the one hand, he made it a point to always believe the impossible. The more outlandish an idea was, the more likely he was to be convinced that it was true. He had finished reading the first three Harry Potter books (all of which were cracking good mysteries) and was eagerly looking forward to receiving his letter from Hogwarts on his next birthday. Harry's letter had been delivered to him when he had turned eleven too, and Ashwin couldn't think of any reason why the same wouldn't happen to him.

On the other hand, this solution was too perfect to be real. If he could summon a djinni, his problem would be solved—he wouldn't have to come up with ideas to earn money for the trip any more. But from all the stories he had read and watched, Ashwin knew there was no such thing as a perfect solution. The heroes always had many problems thrown their way—unless, of course, it was a really boring story. If he was in a really boring story, these instructions would turn out to be a dud and the book would turn out to be a fake.

The book!

Ashwin picked up the purple book and held it carefully. If he *were* to try and summon a djinni—not that he had made up his mind or anything; this could all just be a sham . . . but if he *did* try (even if only to prove the spell was a fake)—he figured it was probably a good idea to read the book and find out what he was in for. He hadn't forgotten the warning at the bottom of the page.

Ashwin spent the rest of the day and half of Monday reading *Adventures among the Djinn* from cover to cover. Mrs Kamath was thrilled to see her son taking a break

from his beloved detectives, and smiled indulgently when he had his nose buried in the book all through dinner.

The more Ashwin read, the more he started to think that the book could be telling him the truth. After all, who would go to all the trouble of making so many things up?

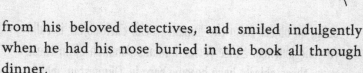

> In Djinnestan, djinn take the form of shadows and smokeless fire. In the human world, they are shape-shifters. Depending on their level and ability, they can take the form of insects, birds, animals and people.

Ashwin went hunting for insects around his house to figure out if he could tell the difference between a real insect and an insect in disguise. In the kitchen, he spotted a line of ants marching towards the window and spent fifteen minutes staring at them. But they all looked the same to him.

He then remembered the lizard in the living room that made his mother shudder in horror every time she spotted it. He looked for it everywhere, but there was no sign of the reptile.

> Djinn can visit the human world in two ways—either they are summoned by a human or they cast a spell and travel

using an object from the human world. Each object is valid for one journey. Since fewer humans summon djinn these days, these objects have become rare in Djinnestan, which, in turn, means very few djinn are able to visit the human world on their own.

'Does that mean that whenever humans lose something, it's because a djinni has actually taken it to Djinnestan to use as a return ticket?' Ashwin exclaimed in indignation, before remembering he only half believed that djinn existed in the first place.

He paid careful attention to the part about summoning djinn.

When a human summons a djinni, the djinni is required to complete one task before he or she can return home.

The djinn who visit the human world without being summoned are only allowed to remain for twenty-four hours. This rule only changes when a human discovers the visiting djinni and binds him or her to the human world. This doesn't happen very often since djinn are masters of disguise.

Djinn can also be forcibly expelled from the human world. If the spell is used on a visiting djinni, they return to their world. If it is used on a summoned djinni, they return to the human who summoned them.

Ashwin read the book two times before he was satisfied that he wasn't going to meet a djinni (*if* he ever met a djinni) completely unprepared. His next mission was to gather all the items for the summoning spell. He was going to try the spell the next day, after his mother left for work. He thought he should spend the rest of Monday getting everything he needed ready.

There was a mirror in his mother's room, but he thought it would be safer to use the one over the washbasin. He was sure he could detach the mirror from the wall and carry it to his room.

The idea of his mother wearing black lipstick was so preposterous that he instantly started thinking of other options. A black marker would be difficult to erase from the mirror and black paint would be messy. Finally he decided that his mom wouldn't mind if he borrowed her black kajal pencil.

'Better some used kajal than a useless mirror,' he reasoned.

He phoned his mother to ask her what incense meant.

'Agarbatti, Ashu,' Mrs Kamath replied. 'I place one beside Ganpati's photo every morning.'

'Oh, why didn't they just say agarbatti, then!' Ashu exclaimed. 'The book I'm reading, I mean. Will you also get some chalk on your way back?'

'Chalk? What for? Did you see a cockroach again? I think there's some Laxman Rekha chalk in the cupboard. That'll take care of the roaches.'

'No, Mom! Just some normal blackboard chalk. I found the board you bought me when I was six. I thought it would be fun to use it again.'

'Okay, okay. No cockroach problem at least!'

'Yeah, our pet lizard eats them all up.'

'Yuck, Ashwin!'

Finding white and red candles was easy enough. His mother kept a box of white candles in the kitchen drawer in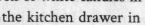

case there was a power cut. He also managed to find a red candle, left over from his birthday party. True, it had white stripes zigzagging around it, but he was hoping the djinni wouldn't be too fussy.

The black candle was tricky, though. Ashwin had no idea where he would find one. He had never seen a candle that colour—

'Oh! The crayon candles!'

28

Ashwin remembered seeing an activity in the craft book he had accidentally stolen from the school library. He flipped through the book and found the perfect solution.

He looked for his art kit, took out the black crayon and peeled its wrapper off. Next, he took the smallest glass tumbler he could find in the kitchen, broke one of the white candles into tiny pieces and stuffed them into the glass. He then broke the crayon into pieces, too, and added them on top of the white pieces.

He put the tumbler in the microwave and heated it until the wax had melted completely. The wick of the white candle had settled in a soggy mess at the bottom of the puddle of melting wax. So he found another piece of thread, stuck it in the glass and waited for it to harden.

While melting, the black of the crayon had blended with the white, and the resulting candle was now a very dark grey. Ashwin squinted and thought it *almost* looked like a black candle. He hoped it was close enough.

Ashwin knew what he would use to bind the djinni. Although his mother complained so much about his mystery obsession, she had gifted him a detective kit on his tenth birthday earlier that year.

He had stashed the box away safely inside his cupboard and only used it on special occasions. The magnifying glass it contained, though, was his most prized possession, and he carried it everywhere he went.

Mrs Kamath returned to find her son drawing stars. He had filled a large sheet of drawing paper with stars of all sizes and had rapidly moved on to a new sheet where he repeated the same pattern.

'What are you making?' She smiled at her son. 'Outer space?'

'Even better,' he grinned back. 'A little bit of magic.'

Depending on their mood, summoned
djinn will try to either impress or
terrify the human who summoned them.
If they are feeling kind, they will take on a
human form which their summoner will be
most comfortable with. However, in their
first meeting with their summoners, most
djinn will try to dazzle them with displays
of strength by taking on a form which
the human is sure to find magnificent.
Some of the more powerful djinn have
been known to appear as dragons or other
fierce monsters in an effort to scare the
summoner into submission.

On Tuesday, Ashwin waited until after his neighbour had checked on him, so he wouldn't be interrupted during the spell. Every morning when Ashwin was home alone, Madhur Uncle rang the doorbell at 11 a.m., usually armed with a snack, and sometimes with an invitation for lunch at his house.

Ashwin clutched the piece of paper with the summoning instructions as he made preparations for the spell. First, he took the bathroom mirror off the wall and into his bedroom. Then he drew a large circle on the floor and placed the mirror, his mom's kajal pencil, the three candles, two agarbatti sticks, a matchbox and his magnifying glass in the centre.

He ran to the kitchen to fill a glass with water, returned to his room and walked around sprinkling water in all four corners. He lit one of the agarbatti sticks, inserted it into the tiny plastic holder on the floor, then drew a large six-point star inside the circle and four small stars outside.

He lit the candles in the prescribed order, repeated the words as the spell instructed, wrote the spell on the mirror, closed his eyes and loudly exclaimed, 'I offer you this magnifying glass as your shelter in this world!'

He then chanted the words again, blew out the candles and waited expectantly, nearly forgetting to breathe.

Nothing happened.

Ashwin waited some more.

Nothing continued to happen.

'I knew this spell wouldn't work,' Ashwin thought grumpily. He hadn't expected to feel quite so disappointed.

Just as he was about to step out of the circle, a haze of purple smoke slowly began to surround his magnifying glass. Ashwin was startled, and his heart slowly began to fill with hope.

As the smoke grew thicker, it whirled around the magnifying glass with dizzying speed. A strangely familiar smell, like the one in the kitchen whenever Mrs Kamath burnt the toast, filled the air. Ashwin felt a leap of excitement in his stomach.

It's working! was Ashwin's first delighted thought.

What will this djinni look like? was his next more apprehensive one. *I don't think a dragon could fit in my room!*

33

Suddenly, he heard a loud bout of coughing emerge from the smoke. Ashwin peered at the purple haze in concern. He wasn't sure what kind of beast coughed at its prey.

'Wha—where am I?' a voice called out from the smoke.

'Uhh . . . my room, O great djinni,' Ashwin answered. He thought it was a good idea to be polite.

'Uhmyroom? What sort of name is that for a place to have?' the voice demanded. Its indignation was interrupted by another round of coughing.

'Ugh, this smoke is horrible!' it complained. 'Can't you do something about it?

'I could switch on the fan, I suppose . . .' Ashwin replied hesitantly. 'And open the window.'

He was about to step out of the circle, when he sensed something moving in the smoke. He turned around to see a figure emerge from the purple fog. As he registered the sight in front of him, his mouth fell open in shock.

'A frog?' he blurted out without stopping to think. 'Of all the shapes you could have chosen, you picked a FROG?'

'Excuse me,' the amphibian sniffed. 'I'll have you know that frogs are amazing creatures. Can *you* survive on both land *and* in water? Can *your* tongue catch your food and throw it down your throat? Can *you* drink water with your skin?'

'Dragons breathe fire,' Ashwin retorted. 'That's much more amazing.'

'A dragon!' the frog exclaimed. 'Turning into a dragon is a Level Five djinn ability!'

'What level are you, then?' Ashwin asked.

The frog suddenly started looking around the room and wouldn't meet his eye. 'Level One . . .'

'Level *One?*'

'. . . is what I will be when I pass out of school.'

'*What?*' Ashwin cried out. 'You're still in school? Can you do *anything?*'

'I can do lots of things!' the frog exclaimed crossly. 'All djinn are born with powers, you know. The school just shows us how to harness them. And I only have three more years to go before I graduate.'

'Okay,' Ashwin sighed in relief. 'You had me worried for a second. By the way, my name is Ashwin. Do djinn have names?'

'You ask a lot of really stupid questions,' the frog said icily. 'My name is Zubeida.'

'Um, sorry,' Ashwin said sheepishly. 'The book didn't say anything about names.'

'What book?'

'The book where I found the summoning spell,' Ashwin replied. 'Or actually, the book the spell fell out of. It's called *Adventures among the Djinn.*'

'Never heard of it,' Zubeida the frog said dismissively. 'So what do you want?'

'Is it . . . is it true, then?' Ashwin had been somewhat taken aback at meeting a frog djinni, and had forgotten all about being excited. Now he was quickly beginning to remember why he had summoned a djinni in the first place. 'Will you grant my wish?'

'I suppose I have to,' Zubeida conceded.

'Before I tell you what I want . . .' Ashwin hesitated, 'could you turn into something else? It's really weird talking to you like this. I never expected a frog djinni.'

'Well, I never expected to be plucked out of my house to be transported to this ghastly Uhmyroom place!' Zubeida looked as indignant as she could, which, under the circumstances, wasn't very much. 'To talk to a boy who prefers dragons to frogs! Hmph . . . typical human behaviour!'

'I don't want you to turn into a dragon,' Ashwin said quickly. 'Aladdin's genie was blue.'

'You would rather talk to a blue-something than a frog?' Zubeida asked.

'Maybe not.' Ashwin began to think about what his ideal djinni would look like.

'I meant to be a hundred times larger, you know?' Zubeida said suddenly. 'I miscalculated. A giant frog would have been terrifying, right?'

'Definitely!' Ashwin agreed. 'But why did you want to frighten me?'

'Well, that's what my teacher says we should do,' Zubeida replied. 'I didn't know who was going to summon me, did I? For all I knew, you could have been an evil human. As a matter of fact, you could still be an evil human.'

'I'm not evil,' Ashwin rushed to assure her. 'I always listen to my mother. Even when she says I have to brush my teeth at night. Would an evil person brush their teeth twice a day?'

'I guess not,' Zubeida said uncertainly. 'I think I could try turning into a human. My teacher says it's easiest to take the form of the dominant species of the world you're in.'

'The dominant species?' Ashwin was perplexed.

'Human beings are the most powerful species in your world, right?' Zubeida explained. 'How that's possible with your puny bodies, I don't understand, but . . . anyway, that's beside the point. Djinn don't need to be taught how to turn into the world's dominant species. The transformation is supposed to be instinctive.'

'Supposed to be?' Ashwin repeated. 'You mean you don't know for sure?'

'I've never been summoned before,' Zubeida said.

'Which means I've summoned an inexperienced newbie?' Ashwin sounded aghast.

'I haven't come here to be insulted,' Zubeida said haughtily. 'If you don't want me around, you can always send me back.'

'No, no,' Ashwin said hurriedly. 'I need you. Turning into a human would be perfect.'

'I thought so,' Zubeida retorted. 'Now turn around.'

'What?' Ashwin looked at the frog djinni in confusion. 'Why?'

'I've never done this before!' Zubeida exclaimed. 'I would rather not have an audience!'

'Okay, okay.' Ashwin turned his back to her. The book was right. Djinn were seriously grumpy.

'You can look now,' Zubeida called out.

Ashwin spun around to see a girl standing where the frog had been. She appeared to be roughly around his age. Her wavy, brown hair was tied back in a ponytail and her eyes were the colour of smoke. She was dressed in a familiar-looking pair of denim shorts and an even more familiar-looking purple T-shirt with a green dinosaur in the middle.

'You're dressed exactly like me!' Ashwin shrieked. 'That's not what a djinni's clothes are supposed to look like!'

'Why not?' Zubeida shrugged. 'Your outfit looked comfortable, so I thought I'd use it too.'

But . . . but . . .' Ashwin stuttered. 'What will people say when they see us dressed like twins? As if looking like a humongous dork is going to help me make friends!'

'I'm not planning on sticking around long enough to find out what people will say,' Zubeida said calmly. 'Tell me what you want so I can go home.'

'You're right,' he admitted. 'It doesn't matter. So . . . you really can grant a wish?'

'Wish away!' she said encouragingly.

'Anything I ask for?' he asked.

'Anything you ask for,' she confirmed.

'Is there any specific way in which I should ask?' Ashwin wanted to know, hardly daring to believe his dream was about to come true. 'I don't want to mess it up. Any words I need to say before or after you—'

'Oh just tell me already!' Zubeida snapped. 'I'll give you anything you want just to get you to shut up and get out of here.'

Ashwin took a deep breath. 'I want some money. Not a *lot* of money. Not like ten crores or anything! But . . . actually . . . why *not* ten crores? I can tell Mom the truth. About where I got it from.'

'Oh,' Zubeida frowned. 'But that's impossible.'

Djinn do not require food or drink to survive, but they eat human food when they take human form. Djinn enjoy rich flavours, smells and other sensations. As a result, when exposed to food in the human world, many djinn find themselves unable to establish control over their eating habits. While some djinn have been known to display allergies to human dishes, a few develop addictions to certain kinds of food from the human world. An infatuation with chocolate is particularly dangerous. Several djinn have fallen into states of deep depression on their return to Djinnestan, which is unfortunately devoid of chocolate.

'What do you mean it's impossible?' Ashwin demanded. 'You said you would give me anything I asked for!'

'You'll just have to ask for something else,' Zubeida said calmly.

'I was mostly joking about the ten crores. Is there a limit to how much money I can ask for?'

'You cannot ask for money at all,' Zubeida said. 'Not unless you want me to steal it for you.'

'What do you mean?' Ashwin was mystified.

'Djinn cannot just conjure money from nowhere,' she replied. 'It's one of the first rules we're taught in school. We're not magicians.'

'You're not magicians?' Ashwin yelped. 'You just turned from a frog into a girl!'

'That's not magic.' Zubeida shook her head. 'That's just manipulating the physical universe.'

'Huh?'

'We can change something that exists,' Zubeida explained. 'But we can't create something out of nothing.'

'So if I tell you to turn my house into a pineapple under the sea,' Ashwin said slowly, 'you can do that?'

'Well, some djinn could,' she said. 'But that's not really your wish, is it?'

'You know what I want,' he said. 'Can't you turn a pack of playing cards into hundred-rupee notes or something?'

'I could. But the money will disappear when I return home. It'll turn back into the cards. Is that your wish?'

'That doesn't count,' Ashwin said. 'If I pass on the money to someone else, they'll miss it when you're gone.'

'So?'

'So, that's cheating!'

Zubeida gave him a strange look. 'You don't want me to help you steal money. You don't want me to help you make money. What *do* you want?'

'I want to go on my school trip,' Ashwin sighed. 'That's what I need the money for.'

'Oh, you want a vacation?' Zubeida looked more cheerful. 'I could take you anywhere you want to go. Let me see . . .'

She rummaged in the pockets of her shorts and took out a small leather-bound notebook. She quickly flipped the pages, muttering, 'Flying . . . flying . . .'

'What's that?' Ashwin asked.

'Nothing!' Zubeida looked up quickly and thrust the notebook back into her pocket. 'Like I said, I could get you there. Wherever *there* is. Djinn are supposed to be able to fly at lightning speed.'

'That won't work,' Ashwin said. 'The reason I want to go on this trip has nothing to do with the place.'

'What *is* the reason, then?' Zubeida wanted to know.

'What else can you do?' Ashwin countered.

Zubeida looked at him suspiciously and turned her back to him so he couldn't see what she was doing.

'With my age and schooling level,' she said, 'I should be able to turn into animals, travel at the speed of sound, fly, mimic voices, influence a person's dream by whispering while they sleep, move items using telekinesis, create illusions to make objects appear different and . . . turn invisible.'

'Are you reading from your notebook?' Ashwin tried to look.

'Of course not,' Zubeida snapped and whirled around. 'Djinn don't need notebooks to perform spells.'

'But none of your spells will help me!' Ashwin exclaimed. 'My book didn't say anything about a djinni's powers having any restrictions.'

'What book?' Zubeida demanded.

Ashwin walked to his bed, pushed his hand inside his pillowcase and retrieved his copy of *Adventures among the Djinn*. Zubeida grabbed the book from him and read a few pages at random.

'This book was clearly written by a human,' she said finally, making a face. 'An ill-informed one at that.'

Ashwin grabbed the book back from her and cradled it. 'It gave me all the information I needed,' he said defensively.

'Yeah, well,' Zubeida didn't look impressed, 'half knowledge is much more dangerous than no knowledge.'

'You know what?' Ashwin was starting to get angry. 'I don't think you know as much as you say you do. All you do is make excuses for things you can't do!'

'What?' Zubeida exploded.

'Of all the djinn I could have summoned,' Ashwin groaned, 'I got the one who doesn't even know how to be a proper djinni!'

Zubeida took out her notebook again and flipped through it furiously.

'What are you doing now?' Ashwin demanded. 'Looking for another excuse?'

'Nope. Just looking for a way to turn you into a cockroach.'

'I thought djinn didn't need a notebook to perform spells,' Ashwin said mockingly. 'Maybe I should just summon another djinni.'

Zubeida looked up. 'You can't do that.'

'Why not? You're completely useless! I'd rather have a djinni who could actually help me!'

'A very smelly cockroach.' Zubeida returned to looking furiously in her notebook. 'Even the other cockroaches won't want to be near you. You'll be a cockroach with no friends.'

'GET OUT!' Ashwin yelled, stung. 'Go back to your stupid home! I don't want you! I'll just get another djinni!'

'YOU CAN'T!' Zubeida shouted back. 'YOU CAN'T SUMMON TWO DJINN AT THE SAME TIME! AND I CAN'T LEAVE UNTIL YOU GIVE ME A TASK TO PERFORM!'

'BUT I DON'T HAVE ANY OTHER TASK FOR YOU!' Ashwin roared.

'THAT'S NOT MY PROBLEM, IS IT?'

Their shouting match was interrupted by the doorbell. Ashwin was startled into silence.

'I have a djinni in my house,' he muttered to himself.

'WHAT?' Zubeida yelled. 'WHY ARE YOU WHISP—'

'Shhh!' Ashwin hissed. 'There's someone at the door. Act normal.'

Zubeida froze. She continued to stand completely still without moving so much as an eyelash, even as Ashwin stared.

The bell rang again.

'That's not normal, Zubeida!' Ashwin dragged her to the main door. 'Just . . . don't say anything weird.'

He opened the door to find Madhur Uncle smiling at him. 'Ashu, I've made biryani. You must come home for lunch. You—'

He stopped, suddenly noticing Zubeida standing beside Ashwin.

'Oh, hello.' He smiled down at her. The djinni stood silent. Ashwin elbowed her.

'Sorry, Uncle, she's a little shy,' he said when Zubeida continued to say nothing.

'You're the one who told me not to say anything!' Zubeida said loudly. Ashwin groaned.

Madhur Uncle continued to smile, though his eyebrows furrowed in confusion.

'So nice to see one of Ashwin's friends,' he said. 'I've never seen you around before.'

'She's just visiting,' Ashwin said hurriedly. 'Which is why I can't come over, Uncle.'

'Nonsense!' Madhur Uncle said. 'There's enough biryani for both of you. Come on. You must be starving!'

Zubeida glanced at Ashwin as he gestured at her frantically to refuse. The djinni stuck her tongue out at him and followed the neighbour to his house next door. Ashwin looked at the two retreating figures in alarm, grabbed his house keys from the living-room table, locked the front door and scurried behind them.

'Sit, sit,' Madhur Uncle said, pointing at the large wooden table in the centre of the room. 'Give me two minutes.'

He went to a smaller table in front of the sofa, picked up the day's newspaper and turned to the second-to-last page.

'Here.' He handed it to Ashwin. 'Here's a new picture-puzzle for you to solve while I get the food ready.'

'What's a picture-puzzle?' Zubeida was curious in spite of herself. She craned her neck to get a better look at the paper.

'You have to solve the mystery by looking for clues in the picture,' Ashwin explained. 'Madhur Uncle gifted me a whole book of these on my birthday this year. I love them!'

'I don't get it,' Zubeida said, mystified.

'It's easy!' Ashwin exclaimed. 'Look, here you have to figure out which of these students cheated on their test.'

'How?'

'You have to look for clues in the picture. Just look!'

Zubeida frowned at the image.

'This mystery would be much easier to solve in real life,' she remarked.

'That's not true,' Ashwin replied. 'I solved it. It's this boy. He cheated. He brought the essay from home instead of writing it in class. His paper has three holes punched at the side but his notebook has four.'

'And this is supposed to be fun?' Zubeida raised an eyebrow.

'Obviously it would be more fun to solve mysteries in real life.' Ashwin rolled his eyes. 'But in real life, only adults solve mysteries.'

He paused. He looked at Zubeida as if seeing her for the first time.

'What?' she asked, annoyed. 'Why are you staring at me?'

'In real life, only adults solve mysteries . . .' he repeated slowly. 'Or kids with a djinni.'

How to Earn Money and Make Friends
by Ashwin Kamath

1) ~~Recycled art sale~~
2) ~~Nimbu paani stall~~
3) A museum of strange things
4) A djinni detective agency

Djinn need to chant spells to tap into their powers. The schools in Djinnestan train djinn on how to harness the different aspects of their abilities. Reading numerous spells, memorizing them and learning to utter them perfectly is an important part of a djinni's education. In rare instances, djinn have had problems using their powers right at the beginning, and subsequently, throughout the course of their education. In such cases, the djinn find it difficult to adjust to life in Djinnestan and either become nomads in their own world or escape to the human one.

'It's perfect!' Ashwin insisted.

'It's not going to work,' Zubeida replied. 'I'm not even sure I understand it. What does a djinni detective agency even do?'

Ashwin had refused to explain his idea to Zubeida at Madhur Uncle's house. After yelling at him for keeping secrets, Zubeida had become distracted by the food. She had stared at the chicken biryani in front of her for a worrying amount of time before she decided to nibble at a single grain of rice.

Ashwin had glared at her as Madhur Uncle looked bemused. When the neighbour had dashed into the kitchen to get the bowl of raita he had forgotten, Ashwin had demonstrated how to eat like a normal person, completely ignoring the fact that Zubeida was neither normal nor a person. She'd ended up loving the biryani so much that she ate three helpings, each time burying her plate under a mountain of rice.

It was only when they got back to his house that Ashwin finally decided to describe his idea.

'We'll solve mysteries, of course!' he said. Ashwin thought his plan was a stroke of genius. He had always wanted to be a detective like all the kids in the books, and here was his chance. 'We'll advertise so people know there's a detective agency in the neighbourhood willing to solve any crime. No mystery is too small for us! People will hire us, we'll crack the case and they'll pay us for a job well done.'

'So you're going to advertise that you have a djinni working with you?' Zubeida asked.

Ashwin thought about it. 'No, I can't do that,' he finally answered. 'Nobody will take me seriously then. They'll just think I'm a kid playing make-believe. Grown-ups find it very difficult to believe in the impossible.'

'But if you don't tell people you have a djinni, why will they hire you?' Zubeida pointed out.

'They won't care how I solve their mystery as long as I do,' he said confidently. 'They don't need to know I have a magical djinni by my side.'

'I'm not magical!' she exclaimed.

'Physical-universe manipulator, whatever.' Ashwin rolled his eyes. 'The point is that you have powers other detectives don't.'

'So what is your task for me exactly?'

'I want you to be my partner in my brand-new detective agency,' he explained. 'And help me solve mysteries until I earn enough money for my school trip.'

'But that could take forever!' Zubeida gasped.

'It can't,' Ashwin said firmly. 'My trip's in five weeks. We have to earn enough money by then!'

'Five weeks!' she groaned. 'I can't remain in the human world for five weeks! I'll go crazy!'

'The faster we solve mysteries, the sooner we'll earn the money,' Ashwin said, refusing to back down. 'And with your powers, it'll be easy! Whenever we have any suspects, you can just turn invisible and spy on them.'

'Um,' Zubeida hesitated, 'I don't think this is a good idea.'

'It's a brilliant idea!' Ashwin said. 'Come on. Show me how you turn invisible.'

'Fine!' Zubeida replied. 'But you'll have to turn around first.'

'Again?' Ashwin rolled his eyes. 'But you'll be invisible!'

'Just turn!'

Ashwin sighed and whirled around. He heard a rustling sound in the living room behind him. The sound of muffled chanting followed.

'I know you're reading from your secret notebook,' he called out.

'I am not!'

Ashwin rolled his eyes again and waited. He started thinking of ways to let people know about the agency. A name. It definitely needed a catchy name.

'Can I turn around yet?' he asked.

'Yes.'

Ashwin spun around to face a perfectly visible Zubeida. 'I can see you.'

'But look,' Zubeida turned her head to show him the left side of her head, 'you can't see my ear.'

'Spying on people isn't going to work with an invisible ear!' Ashwin cried. 'Your whole body has to be invisible!'

'Okay, okay,' she said. 'Turn around again.'

Ashwin opened his mouth to argue, decided it would waste less time just to do as she asked and showed the djinni his back.

'You can look now,' Zubeida's voice called out.

He turned around again to see nobody standing in front of him.

'It worked!' Ashwin was dumbfounded. 'This is perfect! We're going to make the greatest detective duo there ever was! We're—' he paused. 'I can see you hiding behind the sofa,' he said incredulously.

Zubeida jumped up and dusted her shorts without a

trace of embarrassment. She tucked the notebook back into her pocket and said, 'Good detective eye!'

'What's going on?' Ashwin demanded. 'Can't you turn invisible?'

'It's hard, okay!' Zubeida wailed suddenly. 'Everyone else in my class can do it whenever they want. But I only turn invisible when I'm not expecting it!'

'WHAT?' Ashwin yelled. 'What kind of djinni are you!'

'I told you this detective agency wasn't a good idea!' Zubeida exclaimed.

'Are you even a real djinni?' Ashwin exploded. 'Do you have any powers?'

'Of course I'm a real djinni!' Zubeida shouted. 'You summoned me, didn't you?'

'I'm starting to wish I hadn't!' Ashwin retorted.

'I have powers!' Zubeida continued loudly. 'They just take time to work!'

'Like the time you took to turn invisible? By hiding behind my sofa?'

'I CAN TURN INVISIBLE!' Zubeida yelled. 'IT IS JUST A LOT—'

'Oh!' Ashwin gasped. The djinni had suddenly disappeared. 'I . . . I can't see you any more.'

Zubeida looked down at her no-longer-visible body. 'Told you!'

'How did you do that?' Ashwin asked in amazement. He walked over to where the djinni had been standing and thrust his hand forward into what he thought was thin air.

'OW!' Zubeida yelped. 'I'm invisible, not non-existent!'

'You really did disappear,' Ashwin said softly.

'I told you I had powers,' she said haughtily.

'So how does it work?' he asked, his brain racing. 'You couldn't do it with a spell, but you did it when you were angry? Do all djinn turn invisible when they're mad?'

'No,' Zubeida said despondently. 'I'm supposed to be able to control it by now. But I can't!'

'So all I have to do to get you to turn invisible is make you angry?' he asked. 'That should be easy!'

Zubeida rolled her eyes. Too bad Ashwin couldn't see them.

'So how do you become visible again?' he asked curiously.

'Oh, I'll reappear when I'm not thinking about it,' she said. 'So you think this detective agency thing can really work?'

'Yeah!' Ashwin said enthusiastically. 'We'll design posters to tell people about our agency. I can ask my mother to make copies of them in her office. And I can ask her to help spread the word too. She can put it up on the Internet or something. And she can—' he stopped, suddenly realizing the flaw in his plan.

'She can what?' she prompted.

'What are we going to tell Mom about you?' he asked.

'The truth?' Zubeida answered as if it were the most obvious thing to do.

'But adults are weird,' he said. 'Mom is cooler than most, but I don't know if even she would understand.'

'I don't see what the big deal is,' she said. 'Adult humans would summon djinn all the time, centuries ago.'

'That was then,' he said. 'This is now. Most people don't believe in such things any more. Sometimes it's better not to tell grown-ups about important things. The less they know, the less they'll worry.'

'If you say so.' Zubeida sounded doubtful. 'But what will you tell her?'

'We can tell her you're here on a holiday,' Ashwin replied. 'That you're visiting someone in the building. That's not a complete lie.'

'And what happens when she expects me to go back home to the-someone-I'm-visiting?' Zubeida raised her invisible eyebrows.

'Um . . .' Ashwin thought for a minute. 'You can stay here. But you'll have to turn invisible, or into an ant or something. So she doesn't know you're here.'

'This is *so* not going to work,' Zubeida said.

'We'll worry about that later,' Ashwin said, ignoring the voice in his head that agreed with her. 'Let's focus on our detective agency. First, we need a name. What should we call it?'

'The Dazzling Detective Duo!' Zubeida suggested.

'We're not a circus act.' Ashwin shook his head. 'How about The Mystery Machine?'

'Oh, so we're an appliance now?' Zubeida asked sarcastically. 'What about The UnDetectives Company— to throw off suspicion?'

'We want people to *know* we're detectives, Zubeida.' Ashwin tried very hard not to sound annoyed. 'Maybe we can keep it simple. Something with our names in it?'

'The Zubeida and Ashwin Detective Company?' Zubeida made a face. 'Or, or! How about the A–Z Detective Agency?'

Ashwin's eyes lit up. 'That's perfect!'

Djinnestan exists in a universe parallel
to the human one. While it occupies
a separate space from the human world, it
is essentially the same planet on another
plane. The two worlds coexist. When
a human summons a djinni, the djinni
closest to the human in the parallel world
of Djinnestan appears. That is, unless
a specific djinni has been named in the
summoning spell. This is why some djinn
prefer to live in the remotest areas of
Djinnestan, so that the chances of being
summoned to the human world decrease.

Ashwin and Zubeida spent the rest of the day coming up
with the text for their poster. It wouldn't have taken as
much time as it did if the two hadn't argued over every
second word. In the middle of their quarrel, Zubeida
suddenly turned visible again, which was a huge relief
to Ashwin because he hadn't been sure whether he was
yelling at the djinni or at the curtain.

But finally, just before Mrs Kamath was due to return,
they stopped arguing long enough to have a design ready.
Zubeida didn't want to write, a wish Ashwin was happy to
go along with when he noticed her handwriting looked like
chicken scratch. But she insisted on being allowed to colour.
She was very fascinated by Ashwin's watercolours and
crayons, never having seen anything like them in her world.

'How does it look?' asked Ashwin, laying the poster on
the floor for it to dry. His left cheek was streaked with a
yellow stripe from when Zubeida had attacked him with a
paintbrush for breathing too loudly.

Zubeida and Ashwin both stared at it and privately thought it would have looked much better if all their ideas had been used.

'Not bad,' Zubeida shrugged. 'Can I paint the wall now?'

'Not unless you want to be killed by my mother,' Ashwin retorted. 'Or our supremely strict landlady.'

'Humans can't kill a djinni so easily,' she said. 'We live lives which are ten times longer than human ones.'

'Really?' he asked. 'I thought djinn were immortal.'

'Another fantastic idea from your all-knowing book, I suppose.' Zubeida rolled her eyes. 'I bet I could write a better version. A more accurate version, at any rate.'

Ashwin opened his mouth to say that she would need to include a translation so people would understand her code-like writing, but he suddenly remembered something. He ran to his room and came out with the torn page containing the summoning spell.

'What do you think of this?' he asked, showing her the spell and pointing to the notes in the margins.

Zubeida scanned through the page and her eyes widened. 'This is the spell you used?' she asked, staring at Ashwin. 'To summon me?'

'Yeah.' Ashwin glanced at the spell. 'These handwritten instructions were nearly as useful as the printed ones.'

'Well, at least *this* person knew what they were talking about,' Zubeida said. 'But this spell is very valuable. Aren't you afraid I'm going to destroy it?'

Ashwin shrugged. 'I think you're one of those in-between djinn.'

Zubeida looked at him for a minute, momentarily speechless. She had been taught that most humans thought djinn were untrustworthy and were always trying to control them. But Ashwin seemed to believe she was better than the spell-writer had suggested. Maybe he wasn't like most humans.

'Besides, I've written it all down in my notebook,' Ashwin broke in.

Zubeida sighed. Then again, he probably was.

Ashwin resolved to correct the errors in his copy of *Adventures among the Djinn* that very night. He wondered if his notes, amended with information from a real-life djinni, would eventually go on to help someone else.

His thoughts were interrupted by the sound of keys jingling outside the front door. His mother never rang the doorbell. Sometimes Ashwin was so distracted by what he was working on that he wouldn't even notice the door opening. So his mother had come up with this system to test his vigilance—now she always kept trying to sneak up on him to catch him unawares.

'Zubeida!' Ashwin whispered. 'That's my mom! Remember what we rehearsed!'

The djinni nodded.

'Couldn't sneak up on me. Better luck next time!' Ashwin called out as the door opened and his mother entered the house. Her handbag was slung on her right shoulder while a big bag of groceries drooped down from her left hand. Ashwin hurried to take the bag from her.

'Mom, this is Zubeida,' he said nervously. 'She's visiting her aunt in the D wing. I met her downstairs.'

'Hi, Zubeida!' Mrs Kamath greeted in delight. She was glad to see Ashwin playing with someone his age. She had been getting worried about her son's lack of friends.

'Hello, Aunty,' Zubeida replied and bowed formally. Ashwin had told Zubeida what kids usually called their friends' mothers but he hadn't realized he would need to tell her not to bow. He looked at her in alarm while his mother was greatly amused.

'What are you two up to?' she asked, noticing art supplies on the floor.

'Guess what, Mom?' Ashwin said, shooting the djinni an annoyed frown. 'Zubeida is a fan of mysteries too!'

'There'll be no stopping you now!' Mrs Kamath groaned theatrically.

'And we've decided to start a detective agency together!' he continued.

'A detective agency?' his mother repeated incredulously.

'Are you worried that people won't hire two kids as detectives?' Ashwin asked, sounding concerned.

'Of course not.' His mother hastily rearranged her expression. 'The detective agency sounds like a fantastic idea! The two of you must tell me all about it over dinner. You'll stay for dinner, of course?' she asked Zubeida.

'Sure, Aunty!' Zubeida beamed. 'Do you have biryani too? I love biryani!'

'Oh, no, we don't have biryani,' Mrs Kamath said. 'I was thinking of making Maggi for dinner. But I could order some, if you'd like.'

'What's Maggi?' Zubeida frowned.

Before his mother could reply, Ashwin interrupted, 'You've never had Maggi, Zubeida? Forget the biryani. Your life is going to change forever.'

After dinner, when Zubeida had fallen in love with Mrs Kamath's special Maggi, Ashwin walked with her to the door.

'Thanks, Aunty!' Zubeida called out. 'Maggi is officially my favourite food!'

'Come over any time, Zubeida,' Mrs Kamath smiled from the sofa. She had changed into her pyjamas and was settling in to watch her favourite TV show.

'Wow, I've never seen you behave this nicely,' Ashwin mumbled, sounding amazed.

'I'm only nice to people who are nice to me,' Zubeida whispered and stuck out her tongue. 'So what now?'

Ashwin closed the front door gently behind him and stood in the hallway.

'Can't you turn invisible?' he asked softly, grateful that the television's volume drowned out their voices. 'I'll sneak you into my room. You can sleep there.'

Zubeida took out her notebook, turned a few pages and started reading.

'You forgot to tell me to turn around,' Ashwin reminded her. Zubeida wasn't listening.

'Why don't you turn into a butterfly or an ant or something?' Ashwin persisted.

'I'll try,' Zubeida said, nose deep in her notes. She turned to a different page, then began reading the words in a murmur.

As Ashwin watched, the ten-year-old girl's body was suddenly replaced by—

'Is that a sunflower?' Ashwin asked in disbelief. 'You've turned yourself into a plant?'

The plant shook one of its leaves at Ashwin aggressively. He bent down and hauled the potted plant up in his arms.

'I forgot this outside, Mom,' he said, pushing the door open with his feet and walking past the sofa into the bedroom. 'Zubeida got me a sunflower plant as a gift. Just what I've always wanted!'

Ashwin's detective agency!

vidyakamath08@gmail.com

To CC: Me

Yes, you read that right. My mystery-obsessed son has found a mystery-obsessed friend, and together they've started their very own detective agency!

As much as I complain that he needs to move on from his detectives, I'm unbearably proud of this idea. We played chor-police as kids, but whoever thought of setting up an actual company?!

I'm attaching the poster they designed in this email. I promised Ashwin I would spread the word to help make his agency popular.

Do you think you could forward this to anyone who would find as much delight in this as I did? And remember to get in touch with him if you're ever in need of his services. :D

Love,
Vidya

P.S. I must remember to click photographs this time. I have no evidence of his art sale and his nimbu-paani stand, although I still have vivid memories of the headache the police involvement led to!

Vidya Kamath
2 hrs · 👥

I returned home from work last night to find Ashwin and his new friend sprawled on the floor, surrounded by art supplies. When I asked them what they were working so dedicatedly on, they very coolly replied that they'd decided to start a detective agency together.

So my ten-year-old son has teamed up with his ten-year-old friend to open the A–Z Detective Agency (because Ashwin and Zubeida) and they are both very excited.

They've designed this poster themselves. They want to start solving mysteries as soon as possible, so they need all the publicity they can get!

I read so many Enid Blyton adventures growing up, but I never thought to actually start a mystery-solving company myself! Yeh aaj kal ke bachche, I tell you. :D

Full disclosure: This mother has nothing to do with her son's brilliant idea. In fact, I'm guilty of not allowing him to read as many mysteries as he would like. This Facebook post is my way of making amends.

👍 Nirvan Malhotra, Krisha Shah and 72 others   ↱ 17 shares
↶ View previous 20 comments

🔲 **Dennis D'Souza** Your kid is a genius.

   🔲 **Vidya Kamath** Ah, I'm glad you think so too! I was afraid my opinion was severely biased.

🔲 **Keya Mehta** Ashuuuuu!! God, I want to SQUISH him! What did you feed him to get a brain like that???

   🔲 **Vidya Kamath** A steady diet of Maggi and potato chips.

🧑 **Jenny Bhatt** I cannot find my spectacles. Can I hire them to find my beautiful chashma?

> 👩 **Vidya Kamath** I'm sure they'd be delighted. But you're blind without your glasses! How are you reading my Facebook status?

> > 🧑 **Jenny Bhatt** I'm being forced to use my ugly spare pair. Remember the one where the right handle had to be sellotaped after I sat on it? I feel like Harry Potter!

> > > 👩 **Vidya Kamath** The A–Z Detective Agency to your rescue!

> > > > 🧑 **Jenny Bhatt** To rescue my self-respect for sure!

🧑 **Asad Malik** I feel like the poster isn't getting the attention it deserves. I'd hire Ashwin in a heartbeat.

> 👩 **Vidya Kamath** Ufff these advertising agencies are trying to take over the world. Let my son be a detective na! More exciting than copywriter/graphic designer.

> > 🧑 **Asad Malik** You make a good point. Maybe he can hire me?

Djinn living in Djinnestan are unfamiliar with modern technology and rely on their powers for everything they need. Towards the end of their education, djinn specialize in different kinds of magic. Most find the sort of powers they enjoy most, and concentrate on developing them further. Since some djinn are better suited to certain tasks, they have devised a barter system of powers where they exchange tasks they want to perform.

An entire day had passed since Ashwin and Zubeida had formed the A–Z Detective Agency. Mrs Kamath had taken their poster to her office to get it photocopied. There was nothing they could do but wait.

They had spent the day doing nothing of consequence. Ashwin had tried convincing Zubeida to demonstrate some of her other powers, but she wasn't in the mood. Instead, they spent the day drawing, colouring and playing board games. Ashwin taught Zubeida Ludo, Scotland Yard, Monopoly, Cluedo, Taboo and Uno. Ashwin's favourite game was Cluedo, while Zubeida took an instant liking to Uno, and they took turns playing the two games.

Mrs Kamath came home to a pair of furious ten-year-olds. 'YOU USED DRAW FOUR ON ME THREE TIMES!' Ashwin shouted at Zubeida. 'YOU CHEATER!'

'YOU KEPT CHANGING THE COLOUR TO RED!'
Zubeida yelled back. 'I DIDN'T HAVE ANY RED CARDS!'

Mrs Kamath managed to calm them both down by
showing them what she was carrying. She had brought
home a stack of sheets in two sizes—the larger ones were
colourful copies of their poster while the smaller ones
were black and white.

'You can use one as a poster and the other as a flyer,'
she explained to her son. 'I've emailed it to my friends, and
I've put it up on Facebook too.'

'Thanks, Mom!' Ashwin beamed. 'We'll start right away!'

'No way.' Mrs Kamath grabbed her son's arm. 'It's too
late now. You can start working tomorrow. Tonight it's
time to relax. You'll stay for dinner again, Zubeida? We'd
love to have you.'

Zubeida nodded happily. After Ashwin had kept the
sunflower plant in his room the previous night, he had
confided in his mother that Zubeida's relatives didn't seem
to like her much.

'Her parents couldn't take her with them,' he had
explained, sticking to the cover story he had come up with.
'They've gone to America for work, so they left Zubeida
with her aunt. But she doesn't seem very happy there! Her
aunt and uncle think she's too weird.'

An appalled Mrs Kamath had wanted to call Zubeida's
relatives right away to exchange some Very Stern Words

with them. When Ashwin couldn't convince her that it was none of their business, he had to resort to faking a stomach ache in an effort to distract her. His acting had worked a little too well. She had made him swallow two large tablespoons of some disgustingly yellow syrup before she was satisfied. She also insisted that he couldn't eat anything other than curd and rice for dinner.

While Mrs Kamath forgot to check in on Zubeida's relatives, she did resolve to make up for their inhospitality. She had quickly grown fond of the strange little girl and was happy that her son had taken her under his wing.

'I hope you're in the mood for pasta, Zubeida,' Mrs Kamath said. 'We like ours dripping with cheese!'

Zubeida and Ashwin had settled into a comfortable rhythm by the third day. The djinni would spend the night as a sunflower plant and transform into a girl the moment Mrs Kamath left for work. They hadn't planned what they would do on the days Mrs Kamath had a holiday, but they were sure they'd figure something out. The only thing Ashwin had to keep reminding himself was not to grumble and glare at the sunflower whenever the djinni was in the mood for mischief and his mother was in the same room.

'How do we start?' Zubeida asked. Both Ashwin and Zubeida were standing outside Ashwin's front door, each armed with a stack of the photocopied posters and flyers.

'I think we should slip the black-and-white flyers under people's doors,' he decided. 'And we can put up the large, colourful posters in the society and around the neighbourhood. They'll draw more attention that way.'

He made sure he had remembered to carry a roll of Sellotape and a pair of scissors before they set off on their mission. He also had his trusty magnifying glass in case any emergency detection was required.

The two budding detectives spent the morning distributing the flyers in all twelve buildings of the society. At some houses, they found newspapers lying rolled up in front of the door, and slipped their flyers into the roll. They then sellotaped the posters in the elevators and on the noticeboards in the society. Ashwin thought it would be a good idea to hand a few flyers to the security guards at both entrances.

'Only give them to people who don't live here, okay, Uncle?' Ashwin instructed the guard. 'All the houses already have our flyers.'

After making sure that they had gone around the whole society, Ashwin and Zubeida took a snack-and-drink break at Madhur Uncle's house, before venturing outside their society. As they walked out of the main entrance, Zubeida's arm brushed against one of the metal bars which zigzagged across the large open gate.

'OW!' she yelped, clutching her arm in agony.

Ashwin turned around to see the djinni's right arm covered in an ugly crimson rash from shoulder to wrist.

'What happened?' he demanded in astonishment. 'What did you do?'

'I didn't do anything,' Zubeida replied weakly. She appeared nauseous as she delicately held her arm out away from her body.

'Why is your hand all weird and red?' Ashwin asked insistently. 'It was normal a minute ago.'

Zubeida didn't reply but looked at the gate warily. She made sure to steer clear of it as she exited the society and refused to answer any of Ashwin's increasingly puzzled questions. He soon grew tired of interrogating her and decided to focus on their mission.

Their first stop was the neighbourhood grocery store. The lady who owned the tiny store knew Ashwin and his

mother and sometimes slipped him a bar of chocolate after
making him promise to keep it a secret.

'Aunty, can I stick this poster on the wall outside?'
Ashwin asked her. 'Zubeida and I have started a detective
agency and we want as many people as possible to know
about it!'

The lady looked at the poster and smiled. 'Of course, of
course. It looks so beautiful!'

'And can we keep these flyers in your store?' Zubeida
asked, remembering Ashwin's instructions to the security
guards. 'You could hand them out to your customers.'

'Of course, of course!' the lady repeated. 'You kids are
working so hard on such a hot day!' She opened the glass
door of the tiny refrigerator beside her and took out two
boxes of Frooti. 'Here. But don't tell anyone else, okay?'
she reminded Ashwin.

'You're the best, Aunty!' he grinned. He left a small pile
of flyers on the counter in front of her, weighing them
down with a plastic jar full of chewing gum. He then stuck
a large poster on the wall just outside the store.

Zubeida, who had already finished drinking her
Frooti, smacked her lips. 'I love all the food in your world,'
she said happily.

'Why? What do you eat back home?' Ashwin asked,
piercing his own Frooti pack with a straw.

'Nothing,' Zubeida replied.

'Really?'

'Djinn don't need to eat or drink anything to live,' Zubeida informed him.

'You could have fooled me,' Ashwin said, thinking about how much food the djinni had consumed so far.

Zubeida stuck her Frooti-tinged tongue out at him. 'Where else can we stick the posters?'

Ashwin looked around and spotted a familiar face.

'Come on!' he said, pulling Zubeida by the arm.

'Hi, Oz Chacha!' he greeted the homeless man who lay sprawled on the footpath, his arms holding a book over his face.

The man was dressed in his usual outfit: a pair of loose, black pants which stopped just above his ankles, a tattered red-and-white-checked shirt under a faded olive-green jacket. He was in those clothes every time Ashwin had seen him, but they always seemed to be caked in the exact same amount of dirt—never more, never less. Ashwin vaguely wondered how Oz Chacha managed to maintain the same level of dirt, then remembered why he was there.

'Can I ask you for a favour?'

'Do you think I have all the time in the world to go around doing favours for people?' the man grumbled. He lowered the book and looked up to see who had interrupted his reading. 'Oh, it's you.'

'It's just a tiny favour, Oz Chacha,' Ashwin said nervously. Oz Chacha was notoriously bad-tempered, even with people he seemed to like. Ashwin's mother, too, hadn't been able to escape his jibes, but she accepted them cheerfully enough.

'How many times have I told you?' the man barked. 'Just call me Oz.'

'But Mom won't allow me to,' Ashwin explained. 'She says you can't call people who are older than you by just their first name.'

'Your mother isn't here,' the man snapped. 'And Oz isn't even my name. You can add the Chacha when she's around if it will keep her off your back.'

'Okay, Oz,' Ashwin said, the unfamiliar term fitting uncomfortably in his mouth.

'So what do you want, kid?' Oz demanded.

'Well, Zubeida and I . . .' It was then that Ashwin noticed the djinni wasn't standing beside him. He looked around and saw her standing a little way off, staring at the old man on the footpath.

Oz followed Ashwin's gaze and froze.

'Who's your friend?' he finally muttered, giving Zubeida a cautious glance.

'She's not my—she's Zubeida,' Ashwin replied.

'Never seen you around before, Zubeida,' Oz addressed the djinni.

'She's visiting relatives in my society,' Ashwin said hurriedly. 'We've started a detective agency together. We were wondering whether—'

'Have we met before?' Zubeida interrupted Ashwin, looking at Oz.

'You've probably seen him outside the society gate, Zubeida,' Ashwin said uncomfortably. 'Oz lives here.'

'I live here,' Oz agreed.

'We were wondering if we could stick this poster up on the wall behind you?' Ashwin requested. 'And leave some flyers underneath so that anyone who wants to can pick one up?'

Ashwin knew that the well-read homeless man surrounded by dozens of books was enough of a novelty that people often stopped and stared at him engrossed in his book. Oz hated the attention, and the audience only made him crankier. But Ashwin was hoping that his detective agency would benefit from some of the attention.

Oz held out his hand for a poster and quickly skimmed through it.

'You're helping this kid with a detective agency, huh?' Oz asked Zubeida.

'We're partners,' Ashwin answered. 'I'm trying to earn some extra money.'

'Don't let me stop you.' Oz threw his arms open. 'The wall is all yours.'

'Thanks, Oz!' Ashwin exclaimed gratefully and took out his Sellotape. Meanwhile, Zubeida kept shooting puzzled glances at the old man. Oz ignored her and went back to his book, stroking his overgrown beard thoughtfully.

'Who was that man?' Zubeida asked Ashwin when they were out of earshot. 'He seemed very . . . familiar.'

'There are lots of homeless people in my world,' Ashwin replied. 'He lives on the street. Mom gives him food sometimes. And books too. He loves to read.'

'Hmm . . .' Zubeida looked thoughtful.

'Come on!' Ashwin said impatiently. 'We've got to put the rest of these up. Maybe we should stick some on the electricity poles. And any more walls we come across. We can't go too far. Mom has a strict border for me when I'm out alone.'

'But you're not alone,' Zubeida pointed out distractedly. She kept glancing over her shoulder at Oz. 'You're with me.'

'A djinni without any powers isn't going to be of much help,' Ashwin said half teasingly, hoping to get the djinni's attention.

'I HAVE POWERS!' Zubeida shouted.

'Calm down,' Ashwin cautioned, 'or you'll turn invisible again.'

'Hmph!' Zubeida glared at him.

'Will any of your powers help with handing out the posters and flyers?' Ashwin asked her.

Zubeida tapped her feet as she thought. 'Telekinesis could help, I suppose,' she said grudgingly. 'But what am I supposed to do with that?'

'Oh!' Ashwin exclaimed. 'You could help get the flyers under the doors of houses which lie beyond my Mom Border.'

'Don't you think people would notice a bunch of sheets flying around in predetermined directions?' she asked.

'Um, you could move them along the ground in a non-obvious manner,' he suggested. 'If anybody spots them, they'll think it's the breeze.'

'Fine!' she said. 'But you can't make fun of my book, okay?'

'Okay,' he agreed. 'But let's go stand somewhere people won't be able to see us.'

Zubeida followed him down the footpath to a spot which was hidden by a wall at the back and a large banyan tree in the front. Ashwin set the flyers on the wraparound cement bench around the tree. Zubeida took her notebook out of her pocket and found the spell she needed. She began chanting as Ashwin looked around to make sure nobody was watching them.

'Oh no!' Zubeida gasped.

Ashwin turned to look at her and then noticed smoke coming from the direction of the bench.

'You set them on fire?' His mouth dropped open in horror.

'It was an accident!' Zubeida yelped.

The flames in the centre of the flyers began to spread. Ashwin dumped half his box of Frooti on the stack while Zubeida used her palms to scoop up some dirt from the ground and poured it on to the fire.

When the fire had been put out, both Ashwin and Zubeida sat on the ground with their backs propped against the wall.

'Djinn use fires to send messages to each other, you know,' Zubeida said hesitantly.

'Don't even.' Ashwin glared at her. 'We'll put up these posters WITHOUT ANY MAGIC and we'll go home.'

'It's not magic—' Zubeida began.

'Shut up.'

To communicate with a faraway
associate, djinn use smoke to send
and receive messages. They can either use
fire to send messages to a particular djinni,
or send a broadcast message to all the
djinn in the vicinity. However, depending
on the presence (or lack thereof) of fire
in the recipient's vicinity, this method
of communication can take a long time.
Many impatient djinn resort to a modified
version of the humans' summoning spell
where they simply summon the djinni they
wish to talk to.

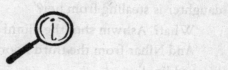

Two days passed without any calls for the A–Z Detective Agency. Ashwin patrolled the phone and kept willing it to ring. But every time it did, it was just his mother checking up on him.

A bored Zubeida spent much of the first day napping and chatting with Madhur Uncle as he fed her all sorts of delicious food. Ashwin, though, was paranoid that the phone would ring the moment he left the house, so he refused to visit his neighbour.

When Zubeida brought over a plate of home-made cake for Ashwin, he seized her hand and yelled, 'I have an idea!'

'Another one?' Zubeida groaned. 'Your first one hasn't worked yet.'

'It will, it will,' he said confidently. 'Mysteries aren't going to pop up just because we want them to. We just have to give them some time. But we don't have to waste our time waiting!'

'Speak for yourself,' she said. 'I haven't been wasting my time at all. I've just had a fascinating conversation with your neighbour. Did you know that Mrs Pilgaonkar's daughter is stealing from her?'

'What?' Ashwin shot the djinni a puzzled look.

'And Nihar from the third floor might run away from his wedding!'

'Who cares!' he exclaimed. He didn't find anything interesting about Madhur Uncle's gossip. 'I think we should set up a haunted house.'

'A what?'

'You know,' he said impatiently. 'One of those houses people walk into to get scared. They're filled with monsters and ghosts and giant spiders and whatnot.'

'Why on earth do you want to fill your house with supernatural creatures?' Zubeida asked, her eyes wide.

'I don't want to—hey! *You're* a supernatural creature,' Ashwin reminded her.

'So you want me to summon some more?' Zubeida asked. 'I don't understand your plan.'

'You would if you'd just sit quietly and listen,' Ashwin sighed. 'The people running these haunted houses charge people money to enter.'

'People pay money to be terrified?' Zubeida asked. 'Humans are weirder than I thought.'

Ashwin ignored her. 'I was thinking that we could turn my house into a haunted house too! The money could go into my trip fund.'

'But how?' Zubeida looked around. 'It doesn't look the least bit haunted. Who will pay to see an ordinary house?'

'That's where you come in.' Ashwin grinned.

That night, Zubeida and Ashwin sneaked out of the house while his mother was asleep.

'You know what you have to do, right?' he asked her. 'Don't mess it up like you usually do.'

'I don't always mess things up!' she protested.

'Set anything else on fire lately?' Ashwin asked. 'Or tried to turn into a giant amphibian? Is transforming yourself into a potted plant considered cool in the djinn world?'

His taunts worked. Zubeida popped out of sight as her rage made her invisible.

'You're welcome,' Ashwin smirked. Zubeida kicked him.

Ashwin's idea was to fake a haunting. He wanted people to believe that his house was genuinely haunted. He would then charge curious people money for the right to

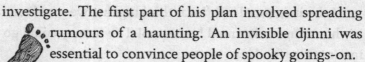

investigate. The first part of his plan involved spreading rumours of a haunting. An invisible djinni was essential to convince people of spooky goings-on.

The two of them had decided that the security guards who made the rounds at night would make for easy targets. An invisible Zubeida would use her powers to mess with them and lead them right to Ashwin's door.

And so, while Ashwin ducked out of sight, Zubeida found one of the guards and began stomping loudly towards him. The startled man turned around, holding his stick up, only to find no one behind him. He looked around, puzzled, then shook his head, and continued walking around the society. The stomping didn't stop and the guard kept shooting nervous glances over his shoulder.

Suddenly, Zubeida howled. The guard whipped around. When he continued to see nothing, he quickly decided he could use some company. He ran to look for Guard Number Two and found him dozing off on the chair near the front gate.

'I wasn't sleeping!' Guard Number Two exclaimed when he was roughly shaken awake. 'I was just resting my eyes.'

Zubeida giggled.

'You don't have to laugh,' Guard Number Two grumbled.

'That wasn't me,' Guard Number One said fearfully. 'That's why I came to find you. I've been hearing strange noises. But I can't see anyone.'

'You need new glasses, old man,' Guard Number Two said unsympathetically. 'It must be Lalchand Madam out on her walk.'

'I didn't see her,' Guard Number One insisted. 'I'm telling you there was nobody there.'

Zubeida chose that moment to emit another howl. Guard Number One clutched his colleague's arm in horror.

'That's just her dog,' Guard Number Two scoffed.

Zubeida decided to step it up a notch. She cleared her throat to make her voice sound as spooky as possible and softly began singing the rhyme Ashwin had taught her.

'Three blind mice. Three blind mice.

See how they run. See how they run.

They all ran after the farmer's wife,

Who cut off their tails with a carving knife.

Did you ever see such a sight in your life

As three blind mice?'

As she finished, she let out a shriek of laughter. The two guards felt their mouths drop open.

'What did I tell you?' Guard Number One whispered.

Just that moment, Ashwin came running up to them.

'Uncle!' he yelled in fright. 'Did you hear that too?'

The two guards flinched when they heard his voice, then relaxed when they saw who it was.

'I've been following the voice from my house!' Ashwin panted. 'I couldn't tell if I was imagining things or not. But you heard it too?'

Both the guards nodded in silent terror. Zubeida began howling again. Ashwin tried very hard to keep his face straight.

'What—what is it?' Guard Number One trembled.

'I think it's the little girl, Uncle!' Ashwin looked around anxiously. 'I heard that a little girl was murdered here fifty years ago. They say her ghost still haunts the society, looking for revenge.'

'What are you doing out here so late, boy?' an unfamiliar voice demanded.

Ashwin turned around to see an old lady holding a leash being tugged by an overly enthusiastic black Labrador. Mrs Lalchand was one of the odder residents of their housing society. She walked her dog Mojo Jojo every night because she hated running into other people—a fate she was unable to avoid during the day. And she wasn't happy at this sudden interruption of her solo stroll.

'Lalchand Madam!' Guard Number One exclaimed. 'Did you hear any strange noises?'

'Strange noises?' Mrs Lalchand looked puzzled. 'No, I've just come out. What kind of noises?'

Before anyone could answer, Mojo Jojo began barking at what looked like nothing. He strained against his leash, trying to pounce on thin air.

'Dogs can sense ghosts, you know,' Guard Number One gasped. He started chanting the Hanuman Chalisa under his breath.

Guard Number Two hurriedly began apologizing to the ghost for not believing in it right from the beginning.

Ashwin smiled uncomfortably. He wondered if dogs could see through Zubeida's invisibility.

Mrs Lalchand tried to get her dog under control. She was a God-fearing woman and firmly believed in the existence of spirits. She didn't want her dog to be cursed for attacking one.

As a member of the canine community, Mojo Jojo could not only see Zubeida but also recognize her as a djinni. He had met her kind before and wanted to be friends with her. But Mrs Lalchand refused to let go.

Zubeida grinned at the dog and whistled, driving Mojo Jojo into a further frenzy. But the eerie whistle turned the adults' blood cold.

'What was that?' Mrs Lalchand asked.

Zubeida couldn't resist. All djinn were fond of dogs. She laughed loudly in delight, then grabbed Guard Number Two's stick and flung it at the bushes. Mojo

Jojo broke free and ran to retrieve it. The invisible djinni ran behind him, pounced on him behind the bushes and began rubbing his belly. Mojo Jojo wriggled happily.

The last thought that flashed through Mrs Lalchand's mind just before she fainted in front of the gate was, *Ugh, I'm going to have to walk him in the day now.*

Ashwin's plan had worked better than he'd thought it would. The next morning, the society was awash with rumours of a ghost. Guard Number Two had resigned from his job while Guard Number One winced every time anyone made any sudden movements. Both he and Ashwin recounted the previous night's adventures to anyone who would listen.

The children of the housing society found themselves immensely fascinated by the thought of a ghost. Many of the older ones claimed to have known the story of the murdered little girl, but had kept it a secret to save the younger children sleepless nights. The tragic tale of the ghost soon snowballed into a complete family history ('My uncle knows someone who spoke to someone who knew the son of the girl's brother'), and involved the place where her body was buried ('Inside one of the thick brick walls of the society. Just like that movie, remember?') and what exactly the ghost wanted ('To kill everyone who reminds her of her murderer').

Mrs Lalchand's door was locked, so all the children turned to Ashwin and Guard Number One to fill in the details of the story they had overheard the elders discussing. Taking advantage of this immense interest, Ashwin told everyone that the girl used to live in the very house he now occupied. He declared that he would let anyone who wanted to explore his house that night in for the very low entry fee of Rs 100. At this announcement, the children dispersed to their respective houses to beg their parents for the cash.

However, before Ashwin and a now-entirely-visible Zubeida could start selling the tickets they made that afternoon, Mrs Lalchand arrived with a man clad in an orange dhoti and ash smeared across his forehead.

After a good night's sleep, the elderly lady had decided she was far too comfortable in her habits to risk having a spirit disrupt them. She wasn't going to be frightened out of exercising her dog at night. She diligently paid the society's monthly maintenance fees—she had a right to some peace and quiet. And she certainly wasn't going to be inconvenienced.

Early that morning, she had phoned everyone she knew to ask for a reliable priest who dealt with such matters. That's how she discovered Guha Baba and set off to fetch him. On interrogating Guard Number One, she discovered the precise location of all the trouble. She appeared unannounced at Ashwin's front door with Guha Baba in tow.

'We are here to exorcise the spirit!' she declared. 'Stand aside, children!' She shoved Ashwin and Zubeida out of the way as Guha Baba walked in carrying a large sack over his back.

Before Ashwin could stop them, the two adults had made themselves comfortable in the living room. Ashwin and Zubeida discovered, in the twenty-five minutes that followed, that exorcising a spirit involved burning a large pile of dried cow dung (which is what the sack contained), non-stop chanting of indecipherable mantras (which Guha Baba seemed to be quite proficient at) and bizarre offerings being thrown into the fire (including a copper coin, a box of kaaju burfi, a long roll of thin metal wire and colourful pieces of paper covered with tiny handwriting).

At the end of the ritual, Guha Baba declared the society free of all spirits, charged a hefty fee from Mrs Lalchand and left without bothering to clean up the charred remains of his puja. Fortunately, he had built a wooden structure, in the middle of which the fire burned, so the living-room floor wasn't damaged. Unfortunately, there were ashes scattered all about the room, one of the walls was discoloured by the smoke and the acrid smell of burnt cow dung hung in the air.

Ashwin sat on the floor with a thud. 'Mom is going to kill me.'

'Come back as a ghost to haunt this society!' Zubeida suggested. 'Now *that* would be a haunted house worth visiting.'

Ashwin threw a cushion at her.

Maya Mehta

Maya Mehta   20:48

Hey, Vidya!

My name is Maya and I work for the Indian Journal.
One of my friends shared your post on Facebook and I
was intrigued. I was wondering if I could interview your
son and his friend about their detective agency. I would
love to write about them for my paper. I'm sure our
readers would find the idea as wonderful as I do. Do you
think this is something they (and you!) would be
interested in?

If you're up for it, please send me an email at
maya@theindianjournal.com with your contact info. I'll be
in touch as soon as I can.

Warm regards,
Maya

Write a reply . . .   ☺

Send

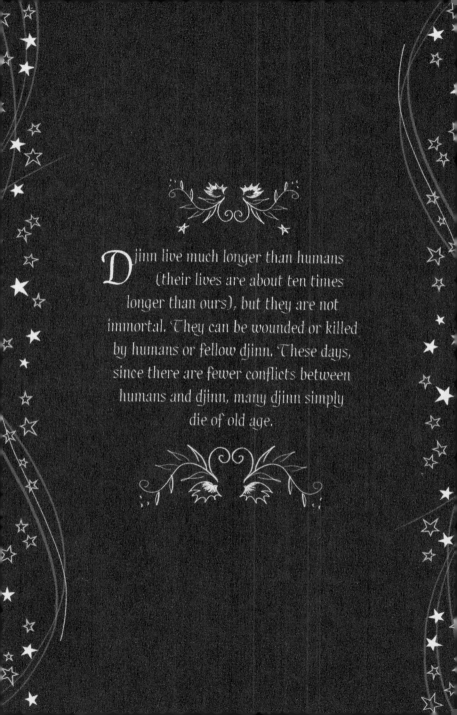

Djinn live much longer than humans (their lives are about ten times longer than ours), but they are not immortal. They can be wounded or killed by humans or fellow djinn. These days, since there are fewer conflicts between humans and djinn, many djinn simply die of old age.

When Mrs Kamath returned to a decidedly unpleasant-smelling house, her first thought was that a bird or an animal had died somewhere a while ago and was only now making its presence felt. Her unsuspecting belief was dispelled by the arrival of Madhur Uncle who brought her up to speed with all that had happened earlier in the day.

Indignant, she had almost been at the door, on her way to demand an explanation from Mrs Lalchand, when she paused, turned around and demanded one from Ashwin first. When Mrs Kamath heard all that Ashwin and Zubeida had to say for themselves (they came clean about their attempts to haunt the society, but left out the invisible-djinni bit), she realized that she had nobody to blame but her too-bright-for-his-own-good son. She declared that the next day's outing to the Museum of Unusual Objects was cancelled and that Ashwin couldn't read his mystery books for a week.

But when Sunday rolled around and the smell still hadn't disappeared, Mrs Kamath realized she was punishing herself more than she was punishing her son. After quickly instructing Ashwin to call Zubeida, she reinstated the weekend trip and resolved to stay out the whole day. Zubeida had never travelled in a local train before, so Mrs Kamath decided to show her the city's famous mode of public transport. Ashwin, who had already been on a few trains, was still discovering things that surprised him with each ride.

'That lady is cutting vegetables!' Zubeida hissed.

'That one is applying make-up!' Ashwin replied in astonishment.

'Many people like to use their time as efficiently as possible,' Mrs Kamath remarked. 'They don't waste the hours they spend travelling in the train on useless things. Like plotting to create mischief and mayhem, for example.'

'But we didn't plot in the train,' Zubeida answered. 'We did it in your living room.'

Mrs Kamath's face twitched as Ashwin frantically gestured at the djinni to shut up. In the light of a new day,

Mrs Kamath was starting to find the whole thing rather hilarious, but she didn't want the two culprits to know that.

Ashwin quickly changed the topic and suggested a game of Colour-Colour. He explained how it was played to Zubeida. One player would suggest a colour as the train reached a station, and the other two would compete to see who spotted the most things of that colour until the next station arrived. The game kept them busy until they got off at Grant Road.

The museum was located in an old bungalow halfway up Malabar Hill.

'This is one of the fanciest areas in Mumbai, Zubeida,' Mrs Kamath said. 'Most people would have to sell both their kidneys, and maybe even a few other organs, to be able to afford even the tiniest flat here.'

'People buy organs?' Zubeida asked, horrified. 'What for?'

Mrs Kamath laughed. 'Never mind.'

Ashwin and Zubeida spent the rest of the taxi ride to the museum discussing what people did with human organs, much to the taxi driver's discomfort.

'Use them to decorate the house for Halloween!'

'Juggle with them.'

'Eat them with soup!'

'Adopt them as pets.'

'Collect them to display in museums,' Ashwin suggested as the relieved taxi driver deposited them at their destination.

A young man, who introduced himself as the gardener, welcomed them into the grounds. Entry to the museum was free but Mrs Kamath had to fill in details about all three visitors in the large register outside the front door. They were the only visitors that morning. Soon all three of them split up, each hurrying to the exhibit that most caught their fancy. Most of the items were displayed on large wooden tables inside glass cases. In front of each item, a handwritten note announced what it was and where it came from. Objects that were too large for the tables were placed in glass boxes on the floor in one corner of the room. The museum itself ran the length of two large rooms at the front of the house.

To get ideas for his own museum of strange objects, Ashwin whipped out his notebook to make a list of some of the things he saw, but he soon got tired of writing and put the book away to concentrate on the exhibits. He walked around with his magnifying glass to take a closer look at some of the stranger displays. The things he *did* note down included:

- an enormous six-foot ball of wool
- a solid-gold toilet seat studded with rubies all around it
- a statue made of hair

- a dustbin shaped like a penguin
- a pair of salt- and pepper-shakers shaped like a spaceship and an alien
- an Ashwin-sized robot made of rubber bands
- a pair of spectacles shaped like a telephone

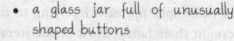

- a glass jar full of unusually shaped buttons
- a large sculpture made out of an old car
- an enormous ketchup bottle that went up till the high ceiling
- a small shelf full of miniature books
- a dollhouse-sized castle made of matchsticks

Ashwin bumped into Zubeida, who was staring at a giant teddy bear dressed like a banana.

'What does that even mean?' Zubeida asked as she spotted Ashwin. 'You are a seriously weird species. Are

102

you sure the planet wouldn't function better if it were run by dolphins?'

Ashwin laughed at her bewilderment and decided it would be more entertaining to explore the museum with the djinni. They spent the next hour walking around the two rooms, commenting on the other bizarre exhibits.

After making sure that they hadn't missed anything, the two of them waited at the end of the second room for Mrs Kamath to finish her round.

'Look!' Zubeida said suddenly. 'There's another door here.'

Ashwin turned around. They had been standing beside a curtained portion of the wall, which he had assumed was a window. But Zubeida had pushed her head under the curtain, then emerged to pull it away.

'Oh, we missed an entire room!' Ashwin said. He tried to push open the door, but it wouldn't budge.

'It's stuck! Give me a hand, Zubeida.'

Zubeida joined him by thrusting her shoulder against the door and giving it an almighty shove.

'I think it's locked,' she said. 'Maybe that room isn't a part of the museum.'

'It most certainly is not,' a voice called out.

Zubeida and Ashwin turned around to see an old woman walking in their direction. She was dressed in a stiff maroon sari, and her grey hair was tied back in a loose bun. An elegant pair of rimless eyeglasses lay perched on her nose. She held a notebook in one hand and a cell phone in the other.

'Oh, sorry!' Ashwin said sheepishly. 'We thought the room had more unusual objects for us to see.'

'The room beyond this one,' the woman said softly, 'has my most prized collection.' She had reached the two and positioned herself in front of the door. 'But it's not open for public viewing. Only *I'm* allowed in there.' She pulled the curtain close.

'Is this your museum?' Ashwin asked in wonder. 'Are you the old lady who threw her house open to curious people?'

A hint of a smile flitted across the woman's face. 'Well, most people call me Mrs Bose,' she replied. 'But yes, I am the old lady you speak of.'

'Wow!' Ashwin exclaimed. 'Your museum is awesome! Where did you find all this cool stuff? My mom read an article about you. It gave me the idea for starting a strange-things museum of my own! I'm trying to earn some money, you know.' He paused for breath.

'I have many sources for my collection,' said Mrs Bose. 'Hunting for unusual objects amuses me. I suppose I should be grateful. There's very little left to amuse an old widow whose children live in different time zones.'

Ashwin shot Zubeida a look. Mrs Bose was addressing them but it looked like she was having a conversation with herself. She didn't seem like she had too many people to talk to. She sounded extraordinarily lonely.

'So you're like a treasure hunter,' Ashwin said, not knowing how to respond.

'Treasure!' Zubeida exclaimed. 'I thought treasure was expensive.'

Mrs Bose smiled. 'The cost of these trinkets is of no consequence,' she said. She didn't speak to the two of them like adults usually speak to children. 'My real treasure is in there.' She tapped the curtained door. 'I suppose I *am* a treasure hunter. And I'm fortunate that I can afford to hunt what others cannot.'

Zubeida and Ashwin looked at each other, puzzled. 'What sort of treasure do you have in there?' Ashwin asked curiously.

'Nothing two children would be interested in,' Mrs Bose said. 'Now why don't we go look for the adult you belong to?'

'I was only asking because I'm looking for ideas,' Ashwin rushed to explain. 'For my own museum?'

Mrs Bose smiled but didn't say anything.

'But I have other ways of earning money too,' Ashwin said when he realized she wasn't going to satisfy his curiosity. 'I've started a detective agency with Zubeida.'

'A detective agency,' Mrs Bose repeated. 'Isn't *that* something?'

'You don't believe me.' Ashwin looked up at Mrs Bose. 'Zubeida, can you show her the flyers we made?'

Zubeida, who was wearing one of Ashwin's old backpacks, slid the bag so that it hung from her left shoulder. She reached into the section in the front and pulled out a thin stack of flyers. They were the last ones left. She handed one of the flyers to Mrs Bose.

'See? We're professional and everything!' Ashwin said as Mrs Bose read the flyer. 'But the thing is, we've not had too many customers.'

'Or *any* customers,' Zubeida added helpfully. Ashwin elbowed her. He sensed an opportunity looming.

'So could we keep these flyers on the table outside?' Ashwin asked Mrs Bose. 'Where the sign-in register is? That way the visitors to your museum will know about us too!'

'I don't have too many visitors,' said Mrs Bose. 'Neither to the museum, nor to the house. It seems that very few people appreciate my collection.'

'Maybe if you displayed your most prized collection, you'd get more people here?' Zubeida proposed.

Ashwin shot her a look. 'Shut up, Zubeida.' He turned to Mrs Bose. 'I'll help spread the word for your museum if you help me spread the word for my detective agency.'

'All right, all right,' Mrs Bose said dismissively. 'You can keep the flyers where you want. I still think they won't do much good, but if it makes you happy . . .'

The three of them soon found Mrs Kamath near the front door. She was on the phone and hadn't noticed them walking over to her.

'Guess what, Mom!' Ashwin exclaimed. 'Mrs Bose has allowed us to advertise in the museum!'

Mrs Kamath smiled vaguely and spoke into her phone, 'Yes, I'll tell them . . . sure . . . no problem. I'll let you know.' She disconnected the call and looked up.

'What did you say?' she asked her son. Zubeida had already walked out the door and placed the flyers under the register. She made sure that the name of their agency was clearly visible.

Ashwin explained his plan and introduced his mother to the owner of the museum. After a few minutes of conversation, which mostly involved Mrs Kamath telling Mrs Bose all about how much she loved the quirky idea of the museum, she finally said goodbye.

When the three of them reached home that evening, Mrs Kamath unlocked the front door and said, 'I have some good news for you kids. Guess who called when we were at the museum?'

'The Prime Minister?' Ashwin suggested.

Mrs Kamath made a face at her son. 'I was talking to a woman called Maya Mehta. Remember how I spoke about your detective agency on Facebook?'

Ashwin nodded.

'Well, this Maya writes articles for the *Indian Journal*. She was very excited about the A–Z Detective Agency. And she wants to interview the two of you!'

'WOW!' Ashwin cried. 'Zubeida, we're going to be famous!'

'What's the *Indian Journal*?' Zubeida wanted to know.

'It's a newspaper!' Ashwin said. 'She'll write about us, and millions of people will read about our agency and we'll get loads of customers! Right, Mom?'

'I don't know about that,' Mrs Kamath replied. 'But it'll still be pretty cool to be in the papers.'

'When is she going to interview us, Mom?' Ashwin asked excitedly.

'Sometime next week, I think,' Mrs Kamath replied. 'It will have to be on a day I'm free. She wants to meet you and she wants to bring a photographer along.'

'We're going to be famous, we're going to be famous,' Ashwin chanted as he danced around the living room.

The telephone rang. Mrs Kamath laughed as she dodged her dancing son on her way to answer it.

'Hello?' she greeted.

'We're going to be famous! We're going to be famous!'

'Ashwin! Quiet! I can't hear anything!'

Ashwin mouthed the words and continued dancing around the room.

'Hello? Sorry, can you say that again? I didn't hear you.'

Mrs Kamath listened for a moment, then turned around to Ashwin and Zubeida with a broad grin.

'It's a call for the A–Z Detective Agency.'

Different types of djinn inhabit different parts of Djinnestan. Most djinn aren't exploratory by nature, so they're quite happy living in the same place——when they haven't been summoned to the human world. However, there are certain nomadic djinn, who are constant travellers without a true home. These djinn tend to be more comfortable in the human world, since they are curious and love to explore.

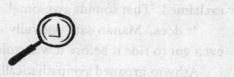

'Can you describe your bicycle?' Ashwin asked. He opened his notebook to write down Manan's response. 'Anything you can remember will help.'

The A–Z Detective Agency's very first case involved a stolen bicycle. A thrilled Ashwin had wanted to go question his client the moment he got off the phone on Sunday night. But Mrs Kamath had refused to allow her son to solve mysteries at such an unearthly hour. She wasn't moved by Ashwin's pleas that detectives often had to work past their bedtime.

Monday morning saw Ashwin and Zubeida meet fourteen-year-old Manan who lived in Ashwin's housing society.

'It has a mint-green body and small, black wheels,' Manan described. 'The wheels are smaller than in normal bicycles because the bike can be folded down to half its size. The rest of the body is also closer to the ground than normal cycles. So the rods for the seat and the handlebars look a bit like giraffe necks.'

'A folding bicycle with giraffe necks!' Ashwin exclaimed. 'That sounds awesome!'

'It does,' Manan said wistfully. 'It was a gift. I barely even got to ride it before it was stolen.'

Ashwin groaned sympathetically. 'And where did you see it last?'

'I had chained it to the tree outside my building on Saturday,' Manan replied. 'But yesterday, it was gone. I hunted for it everywhere, but couldn't find any trace of it. Then I remembered reading about your detective agency. How good are you guys?'

'Don't worry,' Ashwin reassured his first client. 'We solve every case we take. And your missing bicycle has just been moved to the top of our list.'

'We don't have a list,' Zubeida reminded Ashwin as they left Manan's house after promising to return with answers. 'And we've never solved a case.'

'We will!' Ashwin snapped. 'We have to keep his morale up, you know. Robbery victims are a very nervous species.'

'Right.' Zubeida rolled her eyes. 'So what now?'

'First, we make a list of suspects,' Ashwin said. He sat down on the stairs in front of the building's entrance. Zubeida plopped down beside him.

'Who could have stolen the bicycle?' she wondered.

'It wasn't any ordinary cycle either,' Ashwin replied. 'It sounded really fancy. I don't think you get folding bikes in India.'

'So it could have been anyone!' Zubeida sighed. 'That's not very helpful.'

'Well, it must be someone who can actually ride a bicycle,' Ashwin said, and wrote it down in his notebook under the heading 'Suspects'. 'Maybe somebody saw it and really wanted it.'

'Not necessarily,' Zubeida disagreed. 'Someone could have stolen it to sell it. It sounds like something you would do.'

'Hey!' Ashwin said, offended. 'I'm no thief!'

'Where were *you* on Saturday night?' Zubeida narrowed her eyes at him.

'Sleeping!' Ashwin exclaimed. 'Shut up! I am not a suspect!'

'But it *could* have been a kid,' Zubeida said.

Ashwin nodded. 'Or an adult.'

'That sure narrows it down.'

'He said he had locked the cycle up,' Ashwin remembered. 'So it must have been someone who had access to the key. Someone from his own house!'

'Why would someone from his own house steal his bicycle?' Zubeida asked. 'And he's so stupid. If he could fold the bicycle, why didn't he just keep it at home? It would have been safer.'

'But we wouldn't have had a case,' Ashwin pointed out.

'Okay, this is going nowhere,' Zubeida said impatiently. 'Maybe we should figure out how to get the bike back.'

'Which of your powers could help us find it?' Ashwin thought aloud. 'You could turn invisible to follow suspects and see where they lead us.'

'We don't have any suspects.'

'You can move objects with your mind . . . maybe you could move the bicycle back to where it belongs.'

'We don't know where it is.'

'Having a djinni detective is not helpful at all!' Ashwin grumbled.

'You mean *you're* just not a very good detective,' Zubeida replied. 'We should first try and figure out where the bicycle is.'

'Maybe we should look for clues in the society . . .' Ashwin chewed his lips thoughtfully. 'See if anyone noticed anything suspicious.'

'And then maybe I can practise moving a brain into your empty head,' Zubeida said helpfully.

The two detectives spent the rest of the morning walking around the society looking for any sign of the bicycle. Ashwin was sure that no thief would be stupid enough to hide it in plain sight. But Zubeida was adamant about doing something other than making impossible plans.

Once they had combed through every nook and cranny of the society (Zubeida had insisted on using the magnifying glass to search beneath parked cars since the cycle was foldable), the two detectives had to conclude that the cycle wasn't there.

Their next step was to hunt for clues and eyewitnesses. They began to interrogate anybody they met who was willing to talk to them.

The dhobi hadn't seen a bicycle that fit their description, but he wondered if buying one would make carrying a cycle in the train easier. He delivered clothes to many places across the city. A folding bicycle would mean that the travellers in the train's luggage compartment would be less likely to give him dirty looks for allowing an unwieldy cycle to take up precious floor space.

The maid they asked did not know what mint green meant, and they had to spend fifteen minutes trying to describe the different shades of the colour green to her. She hadn't seen any cycle, but she promised to try mint-chocolate-chip ice cream at the new ice-cream parlour down the street.

One of the drivers had seen a green cycle, but on further questioning, it turned out that this cycle did not fold; it was a second-hand mode of transportation and it belonged to his son. The detectives did not think that the driver was trying to be very helpful.

 A small boy claimed to have seen a folding green bicycle being ridden around by a 'big girl'. But he was also convinced that the cycle folded because it had magic powers, so Ashwin didn't know how much to trust his eyewitness account. He added 'big girl' to his list of suspects in any case, since the page was looking depressingly empty.

The security guard was napping when the two found him, and he sleepily assured them that he hadn't noticed anything suspicious. Ashwin doubted he would have realized anything even if the bicycle thief had flown over his head.

Mrs Lalchand had not seen the stolen bicycle but she offered Guha Baba's services in retrieving the stolen vehicle. 'He knows lots of powerful mantras,' she declared. 'They are capable of great things!' They politely declined her offer and ran away before she could insist.

'Maybe we should ask Oz!' Zubeida finally suggested. 'He sits outside the society all day. He might have seen something.'

'He never has his nose out of those books of his,' Ashwin said. But he agreed it was worth a shot.

Zubeida was secretly thrilled. She had been meaning to talk to the strange man ever since their first encounter. But what with one thing and another, she never got the chance to slip over for a conversation. The more she thought about the mysterious aura that enveloped him, the surer she grew that there was more to him than met the eye.

'Hey, Oz,' Zubeida called out. The old man was sitting with his back resting against the wall, his legs drawn up to his chest and a book resting on his knees.

'You're back,' Oz said, looking up. 'Don't you kids have anything useful to do?'

'We're looking for a bicycle thief!' Ashwin explained. 'We were wondering if you'd noticed anything odd.'

'Odder than this one, you mean?' Oz gestured at Zubeida. 'Can't say that I have.'

Ashwin shot Zubeida a confused glance. She was dressed in the same shorts and T-shirt she had worn when she first appeared, an outfit she seemed to have adopted as a uniform. And she still wore the irritable frown she always had when she was with Ashwin. But there was nothing odd about the way she looked.

'What do you mean?' Zubeida asked Oz.

'Of all the places to meet one,' he said, ignoring her question. 'After all these years. Tell me, Zubeida, are you enjoying your vacation in this world?'

Zubeida froze. 'In this world?' she repeated.

'You can't be much older than sixty-five,' Oz said. 'Shouldn't you be in school? What are you doing running around bothering your elders?'

'Sixty-five!' Ashwin exclaimed. 'Zubeida isn't sixty-five years old!'

'Sixty-two actually,' Zubeida replied.

'WHAT?' Ashwin spluttered. 'You're sixty-two?'

'Calm down, it's young for a djinni,' Zubeida retorted. 'We live for hundreds of years. Now be quiet. We have more important things to consider.'

She turned to shoot Oz a triumphant look.

'I should have known!' she exclaimed. 'I knew I could sense something familiar about you, but I just couldn't figure it out. You're one of the castaways!'

'One of the what?' Ashwin asked puzzled.

'If you knew, you would have also realized that we don't like company. Particularly not of our own kind.' Oz went back to reading his book, pointedly ignoring both his visitors. Zubeida bent down and slid the book off the old man's knees.

'You're the one who revealed yourself,' she said. 'You must have wanted some kind of company.'

118

'Unless you're remarkably dense, you would have figured it out eventually,' Oz said dismissively. 'Of course, I can never overestimate the stupidity of my kind. You just surprised me, that's all.'

'Figured *what* out?' Ashwin demanded. 'What are you talking about?' He turned to Zubeida. 'What is he talking about?'

'The thing about Oz is,' Zubeida took a deep breath, 'he's a djinni.'

While most djinn are happy living in their world when they aren't visiting the human one, there are some djinn who voluntarily become castaways. These djinn have given up Djinnestan and have permanently moved into the human world. Such djinn have diminished powers because they are technically under the human's control (even after the human dies), but they live human lives (though much longer).

'What?' Ashwin stared at the homeless old man in shock. 'That's impossible.'

'It is not,' Zubeida said. 'I told you not to believe everything you read in that silly book. Djinn are rare in the human world these days, but they're not extinct. And Oz here is very much a djinni.'

'That was during another time, another world,' Oz retorted. 'I haven't been a djinni in a long time.'

'You can stop being a djinni?' Ashwin asked, astonished.

'Of course not.' Zubeida rolled her eyes. 'He's just being dramatic.'

'And you're being impertinent,' Oz growled.

Zubeida ignored him. 'Castaways are djinn who move to the human world permanently,' she explained to Ashwin. 'They give up their lives in Djinnestan. They trick a human into summoning them and then they just refuse to perform the task assigned to them. That way they can stay in the human world forever.'

'And why do you think Oz is a castaway?' Ashwin asked.

Zubeida tried to think of a way to describe that feeling she had experienced when she first met Oz, of finding him both familiar and a stranger at the same time, like she recognized him from a dream. But she couldn't put it into words.

'I sensed something off about him when we met the other day,' she said instead. 'I didn't expect him to be a castaway, though. He's probably been in the human world for a long time to be unrecognizable to a fellow djinni. And now he as good as admitted it himself.'

'You never told me you were a djinni!' Ashwin turned to Oz accusingly.

'I am not,' Oz said, frowning in irritation. 'Not any more. I've been living a quiet life for decades. I never thought I'd meet a djinni in this corner of the world.' He turned to Zubeida. 'What are you doing here anyway?' he demanded.

Zubeida explained her mission, with Ashwin interrupting to explain why he needed the money.

'A complicated plan for a silly wish.' Oz shook his head. 'Just like a human to think of that.'

'Wanting a friend isn't a silly wish!' Ashwin said indignantly.

'Of course it is,' Oz snapped. 'Friends are too much of a bother. If you knew what was best for you, you'd leave such matters alone.'

'I should have guessed he was a djinni,' Ashwin told Zubeida. 'He's as grumpy as the book says all djinn are.'

'What book?' Oz asked.

'Never mind,' Zubeida said hastily. 'I have a million things to ask you! I've only heard legends of castaways. What's it like living away from Djinnestan? Is it true that castaways were brought up by humans? Which is why they return to the human world? Do castaways run away because they fall in love with a human? Do castaways kidnap human children to bring them up as their own? Do you live with dozens of cats? Will you eventually start talking only in rhyme? Do you really try making friends with pigeons?'

'Make friends with pigeons!' Oz spluttered. 'Of all the outlandish things I've heard! Where on earth did you hear all those absurd rumours?'

'Well, that's what all my teachers say about castaways,' Zubeida shrugged. 'They say Djinnestan is better off without them. They say most castaways are dangerous to djinn-kind. But I always thought the castaway life sounded super adventurous! Better than being stuck in stupid school all day anyway.'

'The ridiculous nonsense they stuff young heads with these days!' Oz exclaimed. 'But I remember quite enjoying myself as a student when I was your age.' He peered at the young djinni. 'You don't like school?'

Zubeida shook her head.

'Why not?' Ashwin asked. He was taking the introduction of a second supernatural creature into his life quite well. 'I think it sounds brilliant! You get to learn to use your powers to do cool things. I wish human schools were that awesome.'

'It's really not that awesome,' Zubeida sighed. 'The teachers don't like me and the other students are mean.'

Oz looked at Zubeida closely. He could sense a shift in her tone and noticed the air of despondency that hung around her. 'How come?' he asked.

'I'm not very good at school, as Ashwin must have noticed by now,' Zubeida replied softly. 'I don't pick things up as easily as the rest of the djinn my age do. And the teachers think I'm being stupid on purpose. I should have been able to master so many powers by now.'

'Like what?' Ashwin wanted to know.

'Like the ones I keep messing up,' Zubeida said. 'It's because of the notebook.'

'What notebook?' Oz asked.

'The one you carry around everywhere you go?' Ashwin added.

Zubeida nodded. She took out the leather notebook from her back pocket and handed it to Oz.

Oz flipped through the pages quizzically. When he realized what it contained, he muttered, 'It's been longer than I realized.' He looked up and answered Ashwin's questioning gaze. 'It's a book of spells. Djinn are born with abilities. But it's the spells that harness the abilities into action.'

'I'm not even supposed to have that notebook!' Zubeida wailed. 'We're supposed to memorize the spells and chant them when we need to. That makes the spells more powerful. But not only can I not remember the spells, I can't even read them properly. I mess everything up!'

Ashwin looked at her in horror. Zubeida looked like she was going to burst into tears, and if there was one thing the ten-year-old boy was mortally afraid of, it was a crying girl. Even if the girl in question was not, in fact, human.

'So what if you need a notebook?' Ashwin asked, desperate to stop the tears. 'You'll learn the spells sooner or later. How does it matter if you need to read them anyway? You can practise reading them perfectly so you don't set anything else on fire. I can help you with that.'

Oz looked at Ashwin with a strange glint in his eyes. 'Humans,' he muttered. 'They never cease to surprise me.'

'I can't show a human my book of spells!' Zubeida was aghast. 'No human is supposed to see them! The djinn rules are very clear about that. Djinn spells are a huge secret.'

'Can *I* tell you a huge secret?' Oz interrupted. '90 per cent of djinn rules are a big fat pile of rubbish.'

Both Zubeida and Ashwin gasped, but for entirely different reasons.

Zubeida couldn't believe Oz had dismissed the rules her teachers—and every other djinni she knew—held sacrosanct. She had never met any djinni with such a casual disregard for proper djinn behaviour.

Meanwhile, Ashwin had just spotted a teenage girl emerging from the entrance gates of his housing society. He didn't recognize the girl but he did recognize the mint-green-giraffe-neck cycle she was riding.

'Zubeida!' he screeched. 'The bicycle thief! Come on!' He grabbed hold of the younger djinni's arm and began dragging her across the street.

A startled Zubeida called out to Oz, 'Can I come back and visit you? I think you're just who I needed to meet.'

'You may not!' Oz said emphatically. 'I need to read five thousand books these humans seem to admire. How am I supposed to concentrate if I'm constantly interrupted by pesky rug rats?'

'Great, thanks!' Zubeida replied cheerfully. 'I'll see you tomorrow!'

'STOP! THIEF!' Ashwin yelled as he jumped out in front of the cycle with his arms spread wide. Zubeida stood beside him to confront the bewildered burglar.

'Are you talking to me?' the girl asked Ashwin after looking around to make sure nobody else was beside her. 'Do I know you?'

'You don't know me but I know you,' Ashwin said coldly. 'A thief is a detective's worst enemy!'

'How about a murderer?' Zubeida supplied.

'A thief is a detective's second-worst enemy!' Ashwin tried again.

'A kidnapper?' Zubeida suggested.

'Third-worst enemy!' Ashwin said less dramatically. 'And that's enough!' he hissed at Zubeida.

He turned to the girl who looked back at him, bemused. 'I know the kind of thief you are! You saw a cool bike and thought, "Oh, this cycle is so awesome. I want one too. I know! Let me take *this* one!" And here you are! Brazenly riding the very cycle you've stolen! Have you no shame, missy?'

'You think I stole this cycle?' The girl raised her eyebrows. 'Um, this is *my* cycle.'

'A crook *and* a liar!' Ashwin gestured wildly. 'Why would we believe a thief? Zubeida! Do something!'

'Like what?' Zubeida inquired.

Ashwin sidled towards her, keeping his eyes on the girl with the cycle to make sure she didn't escape.

127

'You said you could move things around!' he whispered. 'Why don't you turn the bike around? We'll take it to Manan's house!'

'Right,' Zubeida said. She stuck her hand into her back pocket. Ashwin and the alleged bicycle thief waited patiently.

'Wait!' the djinni exclaimed. 'I left it back there!'

She ran across the street, had a hurried conversation with Oz and returned with her leather notebook. The girl looked at the two of them, confused. 'What's the notebook for?' she asked. 'Are you going to make me write "I will not steal things" a hundred times?'

Ashwin realized he would need to distract her to keep her attention off the djinni. He edged closer to the bicycle.

'How did you do it?' Ashwin asked. 'How did you get the key?'

'Am I supposed to have stolen a key, too, now?' the girl asked in exasperation. 'Kid, you're one hundred per cent crazy.'

'Manan told us that he'd chained the cycle to a tree,' Ashwin insisted, resisting the urge to glance at Zubeida to gauge her progress. 'How did you unlock it?'

'*Manan?*' the girl cried. 'Is he the one who—'

The rest of her sentence was interrupted by two loud pops, one following the other.

'What the—' The girl looked down at the tyres of the cycle, then glared at Zubeida who was clutching her notebook tight, wearing an expression of horror.

'What did you do?' the girl screeched. 'Did the tyres burst?'

Ashwin gawked. Zubeida shot him an apologetic look. 'Sorry!'

'Why are you apologizing to *him*?' the girl yelled. 'Who are you two brats anyway? Did my cousin put you up to this?'

'Your *cousin*?' Ashwin managed to squeak.

'Manan! You just mentioned him!'

'Manan is your cousin?' Ashwin stared. 'You stole your cousin's bicycle?'

'IT IS MY BICYCLE, YOU FOOL!' The girl had clearly reached the end of her tether. 'IF YOU ACCUSE ME OF BEING A THIEF ONE MORE TIME, I AM GOING TO SIT ON YOU.'

The threat was alarming enough to compel Ashwin to listen to the girl's version of events. Not that she was in a hurry to provide one. She first demanded that the two explain their actions. Once she understood what was going on, her anger was redirected at her cousin.

'Wait till I get a hold of that rat!' she cried. 'Manan is in BIG trouble.'

It turned out that the bicycle didn't belong to the A–Z Detective Agency's client after all. When Sneha (the girl whose cycle had been a casualty of Zubeida's spell) had showed her cousin the brand-new cycle her uncle had bought her, Manan had been instantly envious. He'd been furious when she had only allowed him to ride it twice around the society. Sneha figured that this was his spiteful way of getting back at her.

'I can't believe he got you two involved,' Sneha said. 'Come on!'

'Where are we going?' Ashwin and Zubeida asked in unison.

'I've got a cousin to kill!'

The A Z Detective Agency Case File

The Bicycle Thief

Victim/Client
Manan Shah

Case
Stolen bicycle

Suspects
~~Big girl   ???~~ Sneha   turned out not to be a suspect,
but actually the bicycle's owner and the client's cousin!

Number of times the suspect kicked the client
Three

Number of times the suspect pulled the client's hair
One

Number of times the suspect tried to punch the client
but was stopped by the timely arrival of the client's
mother
One

Money earned
Zero. Sneha decided that Manan should pay to fix her
burst tyres. Manan decided that the payment would
come from the detective's fees.

Status
Case closed

Current mood
Dispirited

Djinn were much more commonly seen in the human world during ancient times. Powerful rulers often had several djinn under their control. Although a human can only summon one djinni at a time, courtiers would summon djinn on their ruler's behalf and order them to fulfil all the wishes of the monarch. Some of the more benevolent rulers of the past have been known to befriend djinn and have had one as a constant companion.

In the Museum of Unusual Objects, Mrs Bose opened the door of the locked room which Ashwin had been desperate to explore. She frequented the room throughout the day. Mrs Bose liked to be close to her collection and suspected that the objects would be lonely without her. After all, she was their only visitor. The owner of the museum wouldn't give even her maid leave to enter the room, which meant that the room was often cloaked in several layers of dust. The dust would only give way when Mrs Bose, in a fit of spring cleaning, would attack the room with cloth and water every few months.

The exhibits in the room were enough to captivate even the most sceptical of minds. Before she had started building up her collection, Mrs Bose had been a bored, wealthy widow whose children lived on different continents. It was only when she had inadvertently acquired a fossil that turned out to be the claw of an ancient dragon that she discovered a whole new world ripe for her taking.

Mrs Bose now spent her life, and considerable fortune, on tracking down the rarest of objects to adorn her secret museum. No price was too high and no deed too disreputable to stand in the way of what she wanted. The grim determination of a ruthless collector meant that the locked room now boasted of rare archaeological and supernatural wonders.

Among other things, the exhibits included a cursed glove, an instrument used to detect ghosts, a magic Egyptian scroll, a book of ancient prophecies, the shrunken head of a vampire, a haunted terracotta Chinese soldier, the mummy of a witch, the hand of a demon, the horned skull of a gargoyle and a box which unleashed nightmares when opened.

Mrs Bose was standing and admiring a large blood-stained diamond when she heard a cough outside the room. She turned around just in time to spot a dhoti-clad man walking authoritatively into the room, her manservant squawking behind him.

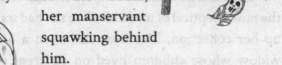

'Sorry, Madam,' the latter panted. 'He barged in here before I could stop him!'

Mrs Bose shot her underling a cold look and dismissed him from the room with a wave. She turned to face the intruder.

'You're early,' she drawled. Her voice hid the unease she felt whenever the shaman was inside the secret room. The way he eyed the objects hungrily sent a shudder of trepidation down her spine.

The man standing in front of her was a shaman gone rogue. Mrs Bose did not know his name. He preferred to be called by the title his profession accorded him—the shaman.

To blend in with the rest of the society he inhabited, the shaman had given up his traditional attire in favour  of a simple dhoti and kurta. The only vestige of his previous life was a tiger-tooth talisman he wore around his neck.

Shamans were supposed to act as healers, guardians of the soul and mediators with the spirit world. But this particular shaman had an axe to grind with djinn. All through his childhood, his father had filled his head with stories of their ancestral wealth. His father claimed to have summoned a djinni when he was younger, who

135

had ended up betraying the family and stealing all their valuables. It was the djinni's fault that the family was now struggling to survive.

The problem was that none of this was, in fact, true. The shaman's father had never possessed any wealth nor had he ever met a djinni. As he had filled his son's brain with lies, however, the father almost began believing his own story. The shaman, in turn, had inherited this fictional hatred, which only solidified in the years to come.

As he grew older, the shaman had become steeped in, and then increasingly obsessed by, djinn lore. The more he read about the djinn, the more convinced he was of their evil nature. He had eventually given up the rules of his faith in order to dedicate himself to becoming a djinn specialist. It was his prime desire in life to find a way to destroy the malicious species altogether.

'Let's go out on to the lawn.' Mrs Bose directed the shaman outside and locked the room behind her.

She shot him a curious look. He was acting quite unlike his usual self. Typically, he would always find excuses to stay in the secret room for as long as he possibly could in order to get a closer, longer look at all the exhibits. This time, not only did he allow himself to be led outside unresistingly, but he hadn't even spared a glance at anything in her collection. Instead, he'd been looking around vaguely, sniffing and twitching his head. She was almost offended by his lack of attention to her precious items.

'What's the status?' Mrs Bose asked him as they both sat down facing each other in the lawn outside. 'Have you arrived early to report success?'

The shaman snapped out of his distraction. 'You know as well as I do that it isn't as easy as that. Djinn are almost impossible to locate these days. Most humans don't even believe in their existence, let alone try summoning one. Modern technology has left very little room for that abominable species.'

'Abominable or not,' Mrs Bose said softly, 'a djinni is what you promised me.'

'I know I did,' the shaman retorted. 'And I intend to uphold the promise. I just need more time.'

'Hasn't enough time been provided already?' Mrs Bose inquired coldly. 'You appear no closer than when you started.'

'There aren't too many djinn left in the human world,' the shaman answered. 'I've told you this already. Djinn can only visit the world in two ways. Either they are summoned by a human or they use an object from the human world which has been smuggled into Djinnestan to act as a gateway between the two worlds. But as fewer humans summon djinn, the number of human objects in their world has also dropped.'

'You said it yourself,' Mrs Bose responded. 'Djinn still exist in the human world. What I fail to understand is why you haven't found one yet.'

'Because even the Visiting Djinn who do manage to enter our world can only stay for twenty-four hours,' the shaman said, a note of exasperation creeping into his voice. They had had this exact discussion more times than he wanted to count. 'And the Summoned Djinn are excellent at disguising themselves.'

'What is the use of your shamanic trances if not to dig out the remaining djinn?' Mrs Bose demanded. 'Isn't that why I hired you? I don't believe I am paying you to make inane excuses.'

Ever since Mrs Bose had stumbled upon an old diary which detailed the narrator's encounters with members of the djinn world, she had thought of nothing else. She was determined to add a djinni to her collection. Unfortunately for her, nowhere in the entire book did the diarist write about how to summon a djinni in the first place.

She had found the shaman through one of her more sordid contacts, and had instantly hired his services. He had shown great expertise in the matter of the djinn; he was well acquainted with their lifestyle and habits. But so far he had proved to be extraordinarily inept in tracking down even the hint of a djinni.

In the beginning they had tried to summon a djinni. For all his knowledge, however, the shaman wasn't aware of the exact spell. After numerous failed attempts, the two djinni hunters had been forced to conclude that capturing one who was already in the human world might be a more promising undertaking.

'I believe you will be pleased with what I have discovered,' the shaman said calmly.

'What?' Mrs Bose was startled. 'You have good news? Why didn't you inform me immediately?'

'I didn't when I came to visit you,' the shaman replied. 'But I do now.'

Once more he craned his neck around, sniffed and twitched. Mrs Bose lost her temper.

'Don't talk in riddles,' she snapped. 'Tell me clearly what you mean.'

In reply, the shaman stood up and walked back to the part of the Museum of Unusual Objects which was open to the public.

'Here!' he said, stopping and gesturing with a flourish.

Mrs Bose looked around and listened. 'I can't hear anything,' she said after a minute.

'H-E-R-E,' the shaman spelled out. 'Here. This is the room where it happened.'

'Where *what* happened?' Mrs Bose asked in irritation.

139

'Where a djinni entered our lives of its own accord,' the shaman said triumphantly.

Mrs Bose stared at the man, wondering if he had finally taken leave of what little sense he possessed. 'You think there's a djinni in this room?' she asked him.

'There *was* a djinni in this room,' the shaman corrected her.

'What utter nonsense!' Mrs Bose rubbished his claim. 'The house has had no new visitors since you were here last week.'

'The tooth doesn't lie,' the shaman said. He craned his neck forward so that Mrs Bose could see the talisman he wore. The tiger tooth had charms etched all around it, which were now glowing faintly.

'It has never done that before,' the shaman explained, 'because it has never sensed the presence of a djinni until now. It grows brighter the closer the djinni is. A djinni was definitely here.'

Mrs Bose wasn't sure whether to be impressed or sceptical. On the one hand, why would a djinni have visited her house without a purpose? On the other hand, while the shaman may have delayed her expectations so far, when it came to djinn, he certainly knew what he was talking about.

She racked her brains for memories of any new visitors or odd incidents that had occurred over the last week, but she couldn't come up with anything. She paced up and down the museum in deep thought for over an hour. The shaman was busy in his own contemplation and didn't look up. It was only when Mrs Bose walked past the front entrance on her way to the lawn that she noticed the flyers advertising the A–Z Detective Agency tucked under the visitor's register.

She paused and pulled out a single piece of paper from the pile. She read the flyer again, then slowly walked back to the room she had left the shaman in.

'Could a djinni disguise itself as a child?' Mrs Bose asked.

'An unusual form,' the shaman said thoughtfully. 'But not an impossible one.'

'Then I think I know our next step,' came the reply.

Most djinn share an uneasy relationship with humans. Neither species wholly trusts the other. Humans eye djinn with suspicion because they know too little of their world and its rules. Contrarily, djinn are suspicious of humans precisely because they know too much of the human world.

Ashwin lay sprawled on the floor of his living room, staring moodily at the ceiling. It had been a week since the bicycle incident but he was still not over it. Not only had his first-ever case been a huge hoax, but judging by the number of people clamouring for the detective agency's services (an impressive grand total of zero), his first client might well turn out to be his last.

What was worse was that he had nobody to grumble to. Zubeida had started slipping off for hours at a time in an effort to become friends with Oz. She only returned in time for lunch. Every time Ashwin offered to accompany her, she insisted on going alone.

'He's more likely to be welcoming if there's only one of us,' she had explained. 'And I *have* to get to know him better.'

Ashwin didn't see how her logic was going to work. Oz had shown no signs of softening. The castaway djinni was always annoyed by the younger djinni's intrusion and had refused to provide her with any more information. But Zubeida was determined to draw him into conversation. Ashwin thought that two people would be harder to ignore than one, but he had stopped asking Zubeida whether he could visit Oz with her.

Ashwin's summer vacation was turning out to be quite disappointing. He was bored and lonely and couldn't think of anything else to do. His detective agency seemed to have flopped with a big, resounding thud and he didn't feel like working on anything else. He couldn't help blaming Zubeida for his current state of affairs. He had never before experienced this feeling of abandonment, and he was starting to realize that an annoying djinni was better than no djinni.

Mrs Kamath had noticed the air of despondency about her son. Nothing she did or said could shake him out of his funk. She finally decided it was time for some drastic intervention.

'I'm going to call Maya Mehta over this weekend,' Mrs Kamath announced during dinner that night.

'Who's Maya Mehta?' Ashwin asked, picking out the peas from the pulao his mother had ordered. He scooped them into a small heap at the edge of the plate. Zubeida gave him a strange look, turned to the takeaway container and meticulously found extra peas for her own plate.

'The journalist from the *Indian Journal*, Ashu!' Mrs Kamath exclaimed. 'Did you forget? She wanted to interview you and Zubeida, remember?' She took the peas from her son's plate and mixed them in her own pulao.

'What's the point?' Ashwin sighed. 'The agency is doomed. Nobody needs us. The one person who did need us was a big fat liar. She'll have nothing to write about.'

'You only got unlucky once, Ashu,' Mrs Kamath said consolingly. 'You can't give up so soon! You'll have plenty of chances to prove what a good detective you are. And having an article in the paper will help more people discover your agency.'

'That's true,' Ashwin said, brightening. 'Maybe we'll get some calls!'

'It's decided then,' Mrs Kamath smiled, happy to see that her plan to cheer up her son had worked. 'Saturday's the day my son becomes a famous detective!'

Maya arrived at the Kamath house on Saturday afternoon, accompanied by a photographer. After a round of introductions, the three adults spent fifteen minutes describing their jobs to each other. Ashwin and Zubeida shot each other looks of exasperation. How *could* they be so dull when there were more exciting things to talk about?

The previous night, Ashwin had conducted a mock interview with Zubeida so she would be prepared for the journalist. He had instructed her to remember not to say or do anything out of the ordinary. In fact, he had reminded her so many times that Zubeida had threatened to turn invisible in the middle of the interview if he didn't leave her alone.

Finally, Mrs Kamath retreated into the kitchen to grab some snacks and glasses of nimbu paani for the two guests. Maya fished out a notebook from her large handbag, sat upright in her chair and asked the two whether they were ready to begin.

'Don't mind Mr Gomes,' she said when she spotted Zubeida staring at the photographer intently. 'We'll just talk to each other for a bit and he'll take some photos of us. Later, maybe we can pose together.'

Both Zubeida and Ashwin nodded and sat next to each other on the sofa. Mrs Kamath emerged from the kitchen bearing a tray. She placed it on the table, asked everybody to help themselves and sat in the chair opposite the sofa.

'I just wanted to tell you how much I love the idea of a detective agency run by two ten-year-olds,' Maya grinned. 'What made you think of starting a detective agency? Where did you get the idea from?'

Ashwin sat up straight. 'I read a lot of detective books and I've always wanted to solve mysteries,' he explained. 'I've also been trying to earn some money during the summer vacation. When I met Zubeida, I thought it would be really cool if we could team up to start a detective agency. We'd have fun and we'd earn some cash too.'

'We've not been very lucky in either department so far,' Zubeida said. Ashwin shot her a quelling look, but before he could stop her, she had told Maya all about their first case.

Maya laughed in delight as she hurriedly scribbled notes. 'Don't worry,' she said. 'You're definitely going to get more cases. I'm going to tell everyone I know about the A–Z Detective Agency. What are you going to do with all the money you'll earn?'

Zubeida shrugged. 'I don't know. Buy a lot of chicken biryani?'

Ashwin rolled his eyes at his partner. 'I'm saving up for my school trip,' he said. 'My class is going to Gujarat before school starts. For a week! It's supposed to be an educational visit but it'll still be fun.'

'Wait, what?' Mrs Kamath interrupted. 'How come I didn't know about this trip?'

'Um . . .' Ashwin hesitated. 'I thought it would be more fun to earn the money myself.'

'Wow!' Maya beamed. 'I've never heard such original reasoning by a ten-year-old before. I think that's a fantastic way to earn some money. And an even more fantastic way to spend it!'

But Mrs Kamath wasn't fooled. She gazed at her son, then abruptly stood up, walked up to the sofa and bent down to hug him tight. 'You're my favourite person, you know?' she whispered.

'You're my favourite person too,' Ashwin whispered back. 'But you're sort of crushing my bones.'

Mrs Kamath laughed, straightened, and dabbed at her suddenly moist eyes. After promising to be right back, she dashed into the bedroom. The inhabitants of the living room distinctly heard the sound of a nose being blown.

Before anyone could comment, the phone rang. Ashwin got up to answer it.

'Do you read many mystery books, too?' Maya asked Zubeida conversationally.

Zubeida reddened. 'I don't really like to read,' she replied. 'The teachers in my school are always yelling at me because I'm so terrible at it. The words just don't make sense to me.'

Maya clucked sympathetically. 'There are many new strategies being used in schools these days, you know,' she said. 'To help students who find it difficult to read or write. You should ask your parents to talk to your teachers about them. You may actually end up realizing reading is fun.'

'*Fun?*' said Zubeida in disbelief. 'I doubt that! But what kind of things do these schools do?' She wondered how the human education system had moved ahead of the djinn one.

Before Maya could reply, Ashwin had hung up and rushed to them excitedly.

'Guess who that was?' he asked Zubeida. 'Mrs Bose! From the museum!'

'What did she want?' Zubeida asked curiously.

'What museum?' Maya asked, just as curiously.

'The Museum of Unusual Objects,' Ashwin replied. 'She owns it. She wants to hire us! The A–Z Detective Agency! She's asked us to meet her in her house tomorrow!'

Maya made a note in her book. 'That sounds brilliant!' she exclaimed. 'Did she tell you what mystery needs solving?'

'Oh,' Ashwin said. 'She didn't. But she said she'll give us the details in person.'

He rushed to his mother's bedroom to give her the good news.

Maya looked after him thoughtfully, then turned to Zubeida and shot her a bright smile. 'I was going to wrap up the interview today and write a small article for next

Sunday's paper,' she said. 'But there's definitely more to the story than just a short interview can reveal.'

The journalist had made up her mind that her readers would not want an incomplete story.

'They'll definitely want to know what other cases you're getting,' she said. 'And how they turn out. This story is now a work in progress.'

'What does that mean?' Zubeida wanted to know.

'It means that you're not rid of me quite yet,' Maya grinned.

Before she left, she asked Ashwin and Zubeida to pose for Mr Gomes, both of them holding up a poster for the A–Z Detective Agency. She then handed both of them her business card.

'It has my phone number on it,' she said. 'So don't be strangers, okay? I'll check up on you in a few days. But if something exciting happens with you two detectives, I'll want to hear. Deal?'

'Deal!'

What Zubeida discovered about Oz and told Ashwin:

'Oz hasn't always been a castaway! He was first summoned to the human world by a librarian. But the man was a strange kind of librarian. He spent a lot of time reading books, but even more time travelling the world. His most important job was to recover powerful books and magical objects for his library. He called himself a guardian of ancient knowledge. You humans and your weird habits!

'Anyway, that's how they first met. The librarian, or guardian or whoever he was, needed a djinni's help to find some sort of evil horn. And Oz was the one he summoned. The two of them nearly died on that quest. But I suppose there's nothing like a near-death experience to bring two beings close together.

'Oz got a kick out of the adventure and decided to stay back in the human world. To make sure that happened, the librarian had to summon him from Djinnestan again. He then asked Oz to count all the stone blocks in the Great Pyramid of Giza. Oz never did, so he got to remain in this world permanently. Then they went on missions all over the planet, hunting for treasures to protect. Isn't that the coolest story you've ever heard?'

What Oz told Zubeida:

'Humans are fools. Which makes them dangerous. Adventurous, heroic and noble humans are doubly dangerous. Steer clear of them at all costs.

'Books are similarly dangerous. The worst kind can change your life. It was a book that got me to the human world. And it is books that now keep me here. I don't know how some humans can stand to read so much. How can they bear to continue their dull, normal lives after reading about such extraordinary ones?'

What Oz didn't tell anyone:

The librarian soon became the djinni's closest friend, something the djinni never admitted to the human. The djinni didn't want the human to become too conceited; he was already insufferably proud of his job and its role in the world.

During the hunt for a lost imperial seal of China in the deserts of Asia, the librarian accidentally stumbled across a conflict zone. On a separate mission in the snowy mountains of Europe, the djinni found himself trapped in an avalanche. The djinni survived. The librarian did not.

The djinni still hasn't returned to Djinnestan. The djinni still hasn't stopped travelling. The djinni still hasn't stopped reading.

All to honour his long-lost friend.

Once djinn began being summoned by people who were not associated with royal families, they became much more common in the human world. Humans still distrusted the djinn, but found them extremely useful. However, an increase in the interactions between the two species meant a greater number of conflicts. The popularity of djinn waned with the advent of modern technology, when humans began to realize that machines were easier to control than djinn.

The next morning found Ashwin and Zubeida being dropped off at Mrs Bose's bungalow, this time by bus. Mrs Kamath had some errands to run before she could return to pick the two of them up.

Mrs Bose was alone when she greeted them and led them past the museum, past her living room and into a large library. The three of them sat in chairs around a small, wooden desk in the corner. She hadn't wanted the shaman to be present. She knew that he loathed the entire djinn species and she was afraid that his dislike would have been evident had he been in the presence of one.

She had a strong suspicion that the djinni had disguised itself as one of the two children. Her plan was to trick the djinni into revealing itself. Once she was sure of the djinni's identity, the shaman could help her trap it for her museum collection.

'How nice to see you again,' she smiled at them. 'I do hope you can help me out of this fix.'

'We were so excited when you called, Aunty!' Ashwin replied. 'I promise that the A–Z Detective Agency won't rest until it has solved your problem!'

'That's very sweet,' Mrs Bose said. 'But first, you must sit down and eat something. Would you like some Pepsi? Or a glass of Rasna?'

'No, no, Aunty,' Ashwin protested, trying to be thoroughly professional. 'Case first, food second.'

'Can we have *both*?' Zubeida asked. 'Rasna and Pepsi? And some food would be super!'

Ashwin rolled his eyes at her. He marvelled at the djinni's insatiable appetite.

'Of course, of course,' Mrs Bose said. 'Whatever you want.'

She summoned her maid and asked her to return from the kitchen armed with fully loaded plates.

Mrs Bose's plot was simple. The shaman had informed her that djinn were severely allergic to pure, unadulterated iron. The presence of iron itself didn't affect them, but if they touched anything made of iron, they began to display a whole host of symptoms, including vomiting, erupting in a fit of red rashes and fainting. Coming into contact with iron also temporarily weakened their powers, since they were too sick to do anything.

Mrs Bose had turned her house upside-down to unearth everything made of iron. She had scattered the objects around the library and in the shelves. She hoped the most interesting ones would attract the children's attention. Failing that, she was sure they would brush against something made of iron in the room. But she didn't want to risk leaving things to chance.

'I wasn't sure whether to add this to the museum,' she said, reaching out to the table behind her and grabbing a small iron statue. 'I bought this from a monk in Tibet. He made it himself and claimed that it was an exact replica of the yeti he'd encountered in the Himalayas. But I wasn't sure whether it would be of much interest. What do you think?'

She held out the statue to be examined by Ashwin and Zubeida. However, Ashwin merely glanced at it and muttered, 'Very nice, very nice!' before opening his backpack and hunting for his notebook inside. Zubeida was too distracted, looking at the doorway, waiting for the promised goodies. Mrs Bose sighed inwardly and replaced the statue on the table.

'So how can we help, Aunty?' Ashwin asked. He elbowed Zubeida to make sure she was paying attention. 'Why did you need detectives?'

'Oh, well, it's quite silly, really,' Mrs Bose answered. 'Do you remember the locked room hidden behind the curtain at the back of the museum?'

Both Ashwin and Zubeida nodded.

'Well, I seem to have misplaced the key to the room.' Mrs Bose did her best to sound flustered. 'I've looked for it everywhere!'

'You hired us to look for a *key*?' Zubeida asked in disbelief. 'Don't you have another one?'

'Only one key, I'm afraid,' Mrs Bose smiled apologetically. 'You must forgive an old woman's paranoia. But I was sure that if I made more copies of it, there were greater chances of it falling into someone else's hands.'

'Can't you call a locksmith?' Ashwin asked. 'He'll be able to make you a copy of the key, won't he? Or even open the door himself!'

'Absolutely impossible,' Mrs Bose replied calmly. 'A locksmith will open the door and be able to see all my most precious treasures. Or, even worse, what if he makes a copy of the key to keep with him? I'll never be able to rest easy!'

'That must be a really special room.' Zubeida shook her head, still wearing a look of incredulity.

'Good thing I have my magnifying glass with me,' Ashwin sighed in relief. 'It'll help us look for the tiny key.'

Mrs Bose took out an iron key from the desk drawer in front of her and held it out on her palm. 'This is the sort of key you need to look for,' she said. 'It belongs to a door which is similar to the locked one. Both the doors were made by the same person.'

Ashwin leant over and examined the key, but to Mrs Bose's annoyance, he didn't attempt to handle it.

'What would you like us to do?' Zubeida asked.

'All I want you to do is find the key for me,' Mrs Bose said, resisting the urge to throw the iron key at both the children. 'I know it's in the house somewhere, because I haven't left the house since the last time I had the key.'

At that moment, the maid walked in with a large serving platter filled with several overflowing plates of food and four glasses of Pepsi and Rasna. Earlier that day, Mrs Bose had handed her an old set of iron plates and had instructed her to bring out the food in those. The kids would *have* to touch the plates while they were reaching for the food.

To Mrs Bose's dismay, however, in her over-enthusiasm, the maid had filled the plates with so much food that the bottom of the iron dishes was nowhere to be seen. She leaned back in her chair in disgust.

'Maybe somebody in your house stole the key?' Ashwin suggested. 'We'll have to talk to them. Everyone's a suspect!'

Mrs Bose nodded distractedly. She wished she had thought of iron forks and spoons. She cheered herself up with the thought of all the other opportunities the room yet offered.

'Where do you remember seeing the key last?' Ashwin asked, poised to take notes. Zubeida was ignoring both of them, too busy nibbling on banana wafers.

'There will be plenty of time for questions,' Mrs Bose said. 'Why don't you eat something first?'

Ashwin shrugged and put his notebook away. He was trying to be as professional as he could, but if the client herself was insisting he feed himself, who was he to argue?

'What do you think of my library?' Mrs Bose gestured around the room. 'Apart from thousands of books, it also houses some of the objects I've collected that don't quite belong in the museum.'

Ashwin's mouth was full, so all he could do was nod in what he hoped was an impressed manner. Full for the moment, Zubeida stood up and walked to the nearest shelf.

'Do you really have thousands of books here?' she asked in awe. 'And you've read them all?'

'Not all,' Mrs Bose said. She was trying not to sound too excited. The shelf Zubeida stood in front of had an iron paperweight in the shape of a crocodile swallowing Planet Earth. 'I buy more books than I can possibly read in my lifetime. But I like owning them.'

Mrs Bose walked up to the shelf and stood behind Zubeida. She picked up the paperweight and carried it back to the desk Ashwin was eating at.

'Do you know what this means?' she asked as she placed the statue in front of Ashwin. 'It comes from an old African myth about the end of the world. But my favourite thing about it is that the crocodile's tail holds a secret.'

She tugged the tail gently. That caused the top of the round planet to pop open.

'A secret compartment!' Ashwin's eyes lit up. 'How cool! Can I try?'

'Of course.' Mrs Bose smiled in satisfaction.

Zubeida ran to the desk to see what was going on. Her knee hit Ashwin's chair and she clutched it in sudden agony. Her book of spells fell out of her pocket with a loud thump. Mrs Bose noticed it and bent down to pick it up, curious to see such an old book.

The djinni's eyes widened in alarm and she let go of her knee. She snatched the notebook and tucked it back into her pocket and out of sight. Meanwhile, Ashwin had turned around in his chair to see what all the commotion was about. As Mrs Bose was straightening herself up, he noticed something dangling from her silver chain.

'YOUR KEY!' he shouted.

Both Mrs Bose and Zubeida looked at him, startled.

'Around your neck!' he exclaimed. 'There's a key around your neck! Is that the one which opens the secret room?'

Mrs Bose cursed under her breath. She made a show of acting astonished and patted her neck.

'You're right!' she said. 'Of all the foolish things to do. I had completely forgotten that I'd hidden the key here for safekeeping.'

Zubeida stared at her. 'You looked around the whole house but not around your neck?' she demanded.

'Oh, you don't need to tell me how ridiculous that sounds,' Mrs Bose said. 'I feel downright silly. Another thing you'll have to forgive an old woman for.'

'Don't worry,' Ashwin said comfortingly. 'My mom does things like that too. Once, she started panicking because she couldn't find her phone while talking to me *on* her phone!'

Zubeida was still not convinced. 'You hired us to look for a key which wasn't lost in the first place,' she said slowly.

'Of course, I'll be more than happy to pay for your services,' Mrs Bose said hurriedly, eager to throw off any lingering doubts. 'You did solve the mystery, after all. You're excellent detectives!'

The thought of payment drove away any suspicious feelings Ashwin might have harboured straight out of his head. Zubeida's own feelings weren't so quick to be swayed. When Mrs Bose offered to treat them both to cold chocolate milkshakes to make up for her foolishness, however, the young djinni found her brain left with nothing more than happy thoughts.

DATE..........

The A Z Detective Agency Case File

The Vanishing Key

<u>Victim/Client</u>
Mrs Bose

<u>Case</u>
Missing key to a secret room

<u>Suspects</u>
Household staff
Visitors to the museum

<u>Culprit</u>
Mrs Bose's faulty memory. The key was around her neck the whole time.

<u>Money earned</u>
Rs 500

<u>Status</u>
Case closed

<u>Current mood</u>
Happily full of junk food

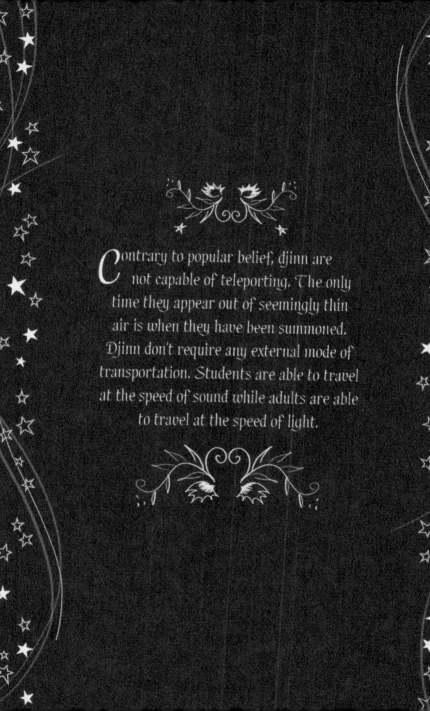

Contrary to popular belief, djinn are
not capable of teleporting. The only
time they appear out of seemingly thin
air is when they have been summoned.
Djinn don't require any external mode of
transportation. Students are able to travel
at the speed of sound while adults are able
to travel at the speed of light.

Rumours that a journalist was going to write about Ashwin and Zubeida soon spread around the housing society, sparking a fresh interest in the A–Z Detective Agency.

For the first time in its admittedly short history, the agency found itself simultaneously engaged to solve not one but two cases. Never having faced such a problem before, the two detectives were not sure about which case they should focus on first. The matter was eventually settled by the toss of a coin, and Ashwin and Zubeida sat down to plan The Case of the Secret Club Intruder.

Earlier that week, a group of seven-year-old boys in the society had asked to speak to Ashwin in private. As he discovered, they were afraid that their Boys-Only Super-Secret Club had been infiltrated.

'And not just by anyone!' Omkar, the club leader had wailed. 'We think a girl is breaking into the clubhouse!'

Apparently, the five boys had set up their club headquarters in a disused shed in the far corner of the society. About three weeks after they had opened the club for business, they had started to notice mysterious changes every time they entered the clubhouse.

While the boys had only decorated it sparsely (mostly with colourful anti-girl posters and banners and warnings that trespassers would be punished), the shed seemed to have undergone a series of small repairs. One day, the leaking ceiling was fixed; another day, the broken glass in the window had vanished; and on yet another day, the walls had been dusted and the floor had been scrubbed clean.

Apart from these changes, the club members frequently found themselves greeted with snacks, bottled juices and heaps of books, where no such things existed before. The five of them had put their heads together to explain the mysterious events and had come to the same conclusion.

'We think the girls have found our secret hideout and want to steal both the idea and the shed!' Omkar had explained. 'They're cleaning up so that they can move in. The books are clearly meant to scare us away, and the food and drinks are obviously poisoned.'

Ashwin's task was simple. He had to find out who the culprits were and inform the members so they could exact a suitable revenge. The five members had pooled in their pocket money to pay a detective. They had tried to discover the identity of the intruder—or intruders—themselves, but every time they'd staked out the clubhouse, nobody turned up. This led them to believe that the girls were spying on them. They figured that a strange, older boy would have much more luck.

'But your partner is not allowed inside,' Omkar had warned. 'And you can't tell her about the clubhouse either. This secret is open to boys only!'

Ashwin, however, didn't want to leave Zubeida behind. You never knew when a djinni would come in handy, even one as ill-equipped as the one he was stuck with.

Zubeida spent the morning practising how to turn invisible without having to resort to anger. Ashwin figured that an invisible djinni would help in case any of the club members were secretly watching their progress.

Ashwin wanted to help the djinni memorize the spell but Zubeida wouldn't allow him to read her book. So he suggested that she turn the spell into a song to make it easier to remember. He turned on the television and switched to a music channel which was playing the latest Bollywood songs. Zubeida picked her favourite one and Ashwin helped her practise the song. The rest was simply a matter of fitting the words of the spell to the tune of the song. In less than an hour, the djinni was able to sing herself invisible.

Zubeida was so excited that she grabbed Ashwin in a hug. Ashwin bravely bore it for a few seconds before pushing her off and reminding her that their task had barely begun. They collected the materials they needed, Zubeida sang and vanished out of sight and the two of them trooped over to the Boys-Only Super-Secret Club.

It was the day of the club meeting, and the intruders always struck then. The plan was simple. In one of the Secret Seven books, Ashwin had read about how the Seven had laid a trap for an intruder by arranging a bucket of water secured to the top of the door. The moment the door opened, the bucket would fall on the trespasser's head.

For this to work, the trap needed to be arranged from inside the room. The two detectives decided that an invisible Zubeida would be inside while Ashwin would hide outside. That way, even if the intruder tried to run away, Ashwin would be able to catch her. To further strengthen their trap, the water in the bucket had liberal amounts of leftover Holi colours—the kind that take days to be scrubbed off the skin—mixed in. And so in case the culprit somehow managed to evade capture, the colour of her skin would give her away.

Ashwin was determined that nothing should go wrong this time around. Both of them got into position. Ashwin crouched behind a parked car and could see the bottom of the door if he peered from underneath the car. Nobody usually went to that part of the society, so he spent nearly two hours with nothing to do. Every now and then, he would straighten up and stretch his numb limbs to give them a chance to regain feeling.

Just as he was beginning to wish he had brought a Secret Seven book to read, he heard footsteps. He looked under the car to see two large feet attached to legs which were encased in jeans.

'Those don't look like they belong to a girl,' Ashwin thought. 'They look like adult feet.'

Before he realized what was happening, there was the sound of a loud crash, followed by a scream of shock. Ashwin ran to the shed just as Zubeida ran out, began singing and popped back into sight.

'What happened?' Ashwin cried.

'It's some lady!' Zubeida shouted back. 'I think the bucket is stuck on her head!'

It turned out that the mysterious intruder had been Omkar's mother all along. She wasn't supposed to know about her son's club, but when she had discovered his secret, she couldn't resist getting involved.

From all the books she had read as a child, she knew that club meetings required snacks and drinks. But Omkar never remembered to carry any with him, so his mother had taken matters into her own hands. She had also decorated the shed with some books, hoping to inspire her son and his friends to pick up a few. While she had been inside, she had taken note of the unsafe parts of the shed and had fixed them up as best as she could. She had given it a thorough cleaning because it looked too grimy for a bunch of children to hang out in.

When she realized why she had been attacked by a bucket full of water, she marched to her son and yelled at him for fifteen minutes. Her skin, having turned an unfortunate shade of magenta, didn't help her mood. Omkar finally managed to slip out to Ashwin's house when his mother was in the bathroom, trying to scrub the vile colour off her skin.

Ashwin was too guilt-ridden to accept the payment Omkar offered. Instead, he suggested that the five members should use the money to buy Omkar's mother a present to cheer her up. The seven-year-old boy thanked him profusely for the idea and ran off to tell his friends the bad news.

Free to focus on the second case, Ashwin and Zubeida had a quick lunch at Madhur Uncle's house, then hurried back out of the building.

Six-year-old Sharvari had been playing cricket with her brother and his friends when she managed to lose yet another cricket ball. Her brother, a teenager, who hadn't wanted her to play with them in the first place, had refused to accept her back in the game.

'He told me that I lost so many balls it was dangerous to let me be a cricketer,' she had told Ashwin and Zubeida heartbrokenly. 'He won't let me play with him unless I find all the cricket balls I lost this summer.'

Even the typically hard-hearted Ashwin had found himself moved by Sharvari's tale of woe. Zubeida, who had taken an instant liking to the adorable six-year-old, had promised to help her.

'How difficult could it be anyway,' she remembered telling Ashwin. 'How many cricket balls can a person even lose in a month?'

The answer, it turned out, was nine. Sharvari had lost nine of her brother's cricket balls in the course of their summer vacation.

Now the two detectives realized that they would have to hunt for the cricket balls the old-fashioned way. Zubeida had offered to attempt transforming scattered stones so that they appeared to be cricket balls. But Ashwin was afraid that someone would get injured if they decided to actually use one of the fake balls in a game.

They had questioned Sharvari about the whereabouts of the various matches she had been part of and details about how she had managed to lose the balls. The six-year-old had quite the talent for misplacing cricket balls.

'If it were a competitive sport, you would have been a champion!' Zubeida had told Sharvari to cheer her up. Ashwin had nodded vigorously.

But the two of them were not quite as appreciative of the unusual talent when they had to look for the cricket balls in the hot afternoon sun. They spent three hours on a seemingly never-ending ball hunt. Ashwin's magnifying glass was of little help in their tracking mission.

Three balls had rolled into a ditch along the inner edge of the society's wall. Two had somehow managed to end up in trees. One ball had found itself in a forgotten corner of the neighbouring society. They rescued the seventh ball from the corner where the stray dog adopted by one of the security guards slept. It was thoroughly chewed up and covered in dog drool.

They discovered one ball in a crow's nest, in an abandoned flowerpot outside the window of a ground-floor apartment. When they went to retrieve it, both Ashwin and Zubeida found themselves attacked by a pair of crows. One nipped Zubeida's fingers, which were clutching the ball, while the other flew at Ashwin's head and lashed at it with its claws. Ashwin felt like someone had aimed a cricket ball at his head. They both ran for cover and found themselves back home.

They never did discover what had happened to the ninth ball. Ashwin decided to sacrifice his yellow foam ball for Zubeida to transform. The djinni picked another peppy Bollywood song to learn and put the spell to music. She then concentrated on turning Ashwin's foam ball into a cricket ball.

It took her a few tries—during the course of which she turned the yellow ball into a series of odd objects, including a bottle, a pillow, an umbrella and, most memorably, a very confused duck—but the spell worked in the end.

Sharvari was so heartbreakingly grateful when the two detectives returned the nine cricket balls to her that Ashwin didn't even mind when she admitted that the only currency she had was mom-baked chocolate brownies and self-made Marie-biscuit-and-Nutella sandwiches.

As Ashwin sat licking Nutella off a finger, he thought about how this was the hardest he had ever worked in a single day, and with no money to show for it at that. But when he remembered Omkar and Sharvari's expressions, he figured that it hadn't been a total loss.

The A Z Detective Agency Case File

The Secret Club Intruder

Victim/Client
Omkar and his Boys-Only Super-Secret Club members

Case
Their secret clubhouse has been infiltrated

Suspects
Girls (Which girls? How many?)

Culprit
Omkar's mother

Number of days it took for the colour to fade from
Omkar's mother's skin
Five

Money earned
Zero

Presents given
A giant bar of chocolate, a bouquet of sunflowers and
a handmade apology card

Status
Case closed

Current mood
Penniless

The A Z Detective Agency Case File

The Runaway Cricket Balls

<u>Victim/Client</u>
Sharvari
<u>Case</u>
Lost cricket balls need to be found
<u>Suspects</u>
Cricketers from the neighbouring society
Crows
The security guard's dog
<u>Culprit</u>
All of the above
Sharvari
<u>Number of scratches Ashwin received</u>
Three
<u>Money earned</u>
Zero. The brownies and the Nutella-biscuit sandwiches
were yummy, though.
<u>Status</u>
Case closed
<u>Current mood</u>
Surprisingly cheerful

There are five different classes of djinn——green, blue, red, black and yellow. The classification isn't based on the colour of their skin, but on how powerful they are. The green djinn are the weakest. The blue djinn are powerful warriors, and they do not like to interact with humans. Each clan of djinn is headed by a black djinni. Yellow djinn are recluses who prefer living away from fellow djinn and don't like to interact with humans either. Red djinn have only one reason to exist——to spread chaos.

'That's it! I have decided. I want to be a castaway!' Zubeida declared one morning.

'Wait, what?' Ashwin stared at her.

'I'm not going back to Djinnestan,' Zubeida nodded. 'Oz seems perfectly happy in your world. I don't see why I can't stay too.'

'But you promised to help me!' Ashwin cried. 'I thought a djinni could only become a castaway if she didn't perform the task.'

'Oh, that's true,' Zubeida said. 'I'll ask Oz if there's a way around that rule. But I think I would be much happier here. No teachers to yell at me. No fellow djinn to mock me. All I have to do is put up with humans.'

'But what will you do here?' Ashwin asked. 'Where will you stay? Won't you miss your friends back home?'

'I don't have that many to begin with,' Zubeida shrugged. 'I'll make new friends here. I have two friends already.'

'You do?' Ashwin frowned. 'Who?'

'You and Oz, of course!' Zubeida replied.

For once, Ashwin thought it would be wiser to keep his opinions to himself. Instead he suggested that the two of them visit Oz right away to ask him what he thought of the plan.

'He'll agree with me,' Zubeida said as the two of them walked out of the building and neared the entrance gate of the society. 'How can he not? He's a castaway himself!'

'We'll see,' said Ashwin. He knew that 'we'll see' was something adults told children when they didn't want to say 'no'.

'Aren't you the two children who are famous detectives?' an unfamiliar voice interrupted their conversation.

Ashwin and Zubeida looked up to see a security guard addressing them. They had never seen him before. Ashwin figured that he had been hired to replace the guard who had quit thanks to their fake haunting.

'We're not famous, Uncle,' Ashwin said, trying to sound modest. 'Are we?'

'Everybody is talking about you,' the guard assured him. 'All the other guards have told me about your detective work. They mentioned you're going to be in the newspaper too! I love watching detective shows on TV. I can't believe I'm meeting two real detectives.'

Both Ashwin and Zubeida found themselves pleased at their new-found celebrity. Ashwin realized that the new guard was a mystery-loving kindred spirit. They postponed their meeting with Oz to discuss the A–Z Detective Agency with him. They told him about all the cases they had solved so far, and he promised to help spread the word about the agency.

'Don't your parents get worried when you're out solving mysteries by yourself?' the guard asked them. 'Aren't they home right now?'

Ashwin shook his head. 'My mom actually helped tell more people about our work,' he said. 'Zubeida is visiting her aunt and uncle in the society, so her parents don't really know what she's up to.'

'Oh, you aren't siblings?' the guard asked, raising his eyebrows in surprise. 'I thought you were brother and sister! What flats do you stay in?'

'I stay in that building.' Ashwin pointed to the building behind them. 'And she stays in that one.' He pointed vaguely at a cluster of buildings on the other side of the society.

'I see,' the guard replied. 'How long have the two of you been staying here?'

'My mom and I have been living here for a few months now,' Ashwin said.

'I arrived a few weeks ago,' Zubeida replied, remembering the story they had rehearsed about her background. 'My parents had to travel to America for some work. They couldn't take me along, so I'm stuck with my relatives.'

'Hmm,' the guard mused. 'I don't think I've seen either of your families around.'

'How could you have!' Ashwin exclaimed. 'You're new here, aren't you?'

'That's true,' the guard replied. 'I am.'

Zubeida tugged at Ashwin's arm and whispered, 'Come on, let's go talk to Oz.'

Ashwin nodded at her and turned to the guard. 'It was nice meeting you, Uncle, but we have to go. See you soon!'

'See you soon,' the guard repeated.

'Wow, I've never met such a chatty guard before,' Ashwin said as they headed out of the society. 'Most of them are usually too busy napping!'

'And did you see what he was wearing around his neck?' Zubeida asked. 'The pendant looked like a tooth of some sort. And it was glowing! A glowing necklace! You humans seem to have done quite well for yourselves even without the help of magic.'

After Mrs Bose had told him about how her plan had failed, the shaman had decided to take matters into his own hands.

It wasn't difficult tracing the phone number on the detective agency's flyer to the address it belonged to. After some subtle inquiries, the shaman had discovered that there was a vacancy for a security guard in the society. He was sure that this was the universe's way of lending support to his plan. There was no way he could fail.

His tiger-tooth pendant had had a constant faint glow ever since he'd stationed himself in the society, disguised as a security guard. But it was only in the presence of the two children that the glow had turned bright. He now knew that one of them was the djinni, but he still wasn't sure *which* one.

After his conversation with them, the shaman observed them for a few days. He was hoping to approach either one of them alone, so that he could see whether the tiger tooth glowed or not. Either way he would know who the djinni was.

Unfortunately, they always seemed to be together, so the shaman couldn't identify which of the children wasn't really human. But he had endless reserves of patience. He had waited for so many years to encounter a djinni; a few more days made no difference to him.

His patience paid off. One morning, the shaman noticed the girl sauntering through the society by herself. He was on duty at the back gate. By the time he found another guard to cover for him—after exchanging break duties with him—the girl had walked out of the front entrance and was in conversation with the homeless man outside.

The shaman stood at the front gate, waiting for her to return, but she stayed outside for a long time. He spotted a tea stall at the other end of the road. He exited the society, went to the stall and ordered a glass of masala chai. As he waited for the tea to be served, he looked over to the man and the girl, but he was still too far away to hear anything.

When he got the glass, he cupped his hands around it and casually made his way to the tree opposite the wall where the homeless man lived. He leaned against the tree and strained his ears but managed to catch only fragments of conversation.

'You're too young . . .'

'How old were you . . .'

'. . . an education is important . . .'

'. . . nobody likes me . . .'

'So many places to explore back home . . .'

The shaman sighed in exasperation. The conversation was making no sense to him and his tiger tooth was only glowing faintly, as it usually did. He was still too far away.

But he couldn't stand too close to them without attracting their attention—and suspicion. He decided to take a circuitous route back to the society so that he could walk past them.

As he got closer, his tiger tooth began to glow brightly. He stared at it and came to a standstill. He couldn't believe that all his years of study had actually borne fruit. He looked at the girl triumphantly.

'A djinni disguising itself as a little girl,' he muttered to himself. 'That's new.'

He realized he was standing in full view of the man and the djinni. Luckily, they were too engrossed in their conversation. He looked around for a hiding spot and noticed another tree. He ducked behind it.

He wondered whether he should grab the djinni now, while it was alone. He looked around. No, there were too many people to act as potential witnesses. He couldn't risk raising a fuss. But now that the identity of the djinni was revealed to him, it was time to hatch a plot with Mrs Bose.

The djinni, who had been sitting on the ground next to the homeless man, was getting up. The shaman watched her bid farewell to the man and head back into the society. The man, meanwhile, picked up the book next to him and began reading from where he had left off.

Before the shaman could wonder what a djinni was doing talking to a seemingly well-read (judging by the number of books he was surrounded by) homeless man, he happened to glance back down at his neck. To his astonishment, the necklace was still glowing brightly, even though the girl was nowhere in sight.

He looked around for an explanation. But found no one there besides the homeless man. The shaman couldn't understand it. He stared at the man. Was the glow a residual after-effect of the djinni's proximity to the tiger tooth? But the last time he was close to the djinni, it had gone back to glowing faintly as soon as the djinni was out of reach.

He came to a sudden realization. He stared at the books scattered on the ground and then at the engrossed homeless man. He remembered that the djinni and the boy had also engaged the man in conversation the first time the shaman had met them. It all made sense.

As improbable as it seemed, the shaman had found a second djinni!

Some djinn have the ability to influence a person's dream as they sleep. There have been instances where djinn have used this influence to trick a human into summoning them. On a twenty-four-hour visit to the human world, the djinni 'suggests' that a human should summon him/her. If the human uses a djinni's name in the spell, that particular djinni is then summoned. The djinn usually pick a human who is susceptible to but not too invested in the summoning. Once the djinni has been summoned, he/she simply refuses to complete the task and lives out the rest of his/her days in the human world.

It was that time of a summer afternoon—just after lunch—when there's nothing to do and everything seems to move in slow motion.

Mrs Kamath was at work and Zubeida was lying down on her stomach on the living-room floor, reading Ashwin's copy of *Adventures among the Djinn*. Ashwin himself was trying not to think about the sorry state of his 'How to Earn Money and Make Friends' plan. He kept shooting the djinni dirty looks whenever the book made her giggle.

'I don't know what you're laughing about,' Ashwin grumbled when one of the more outrageously inaccurate chapters led to Zubeida doubling up with laughter. 'I'm no closer to the school trip and you're no closer to going home.'

'But I don't *want* to go back,' Zubeida pointed out when she had finally stopped laughing long enough to reply. 'And you still have plenty of time for your trip.'

'If by plenty of time, you mean two weeks,' Ashwin retorted, 'then you're even worse at calculations than you are at spells.'

Zubeida glared at him and began hunting through her memory for a spell which would glue a human's mouth shut. Before she could resort to her notebook, however, Ashwin was saved by the ring of the telephone.

It had been several days since anybody had called looking for detectives, so Ashwin forgot his customary polite greeting.

'What?' he barked into the phone instead.

'Is this the A–Z Detective Agency?' a puzzled voice asked. Ashwin realized three things: 1) As hoarse as the voice at the other end was, it belonged to a female, 2) The voice sounded vaguely familiar but Ashwin couldn't place it and 3) he had been very rude to a potential client.

'Yes, this is Ashwin,' he replied sweetly. 'How may I help?'

'I've lost my dog!' the voice cried out desperately. 'Prince is missing and I want him back immediately!'

The Lady—she refused to divulge her name, so that's what Ashwin christened her—had discovered the agency through a friend of hers. She had decided to approach them rather than go to the police because she was sure that they would be able to keep a secret. Apparently, The Lady was a Very Important Person with a lot of Very Powerful

Enemies, and she didn't want any of them to know that her beloved Prince was missing.

'My maid was walking my darling in the park this morning,' The Lady explained. 'And he fought loose to chase a squirrel. She hunted all over but all she returned with was his leash. Obviously, I've fired the careless woman, and I was tempted to have her thrown in jail. But that won't get my Prince back. He's an expensive dog and I can't bear for him to fall into the wrong hands.'

Ashwin rushed in to reassure her that they would make it their mission to rescue Prince. The grateful lady began to describe her precious dog over the phone, when she was seemingly struck by a thought.

'Could you and your friend come over to my house today?' The Lady asked. 'It'll be much easier if I can just show you Prince's photo.'

'My mother's at work,' Ashwin replied. 'But I suppose we could come over in the evening. I can ask her to drop us to your house once she's back.'

'I can't wait till the evening!' The Lady exclaimed. 'Who knows what ordeals Prince will have faced until then.'

'Maybe you could come over to my house?' Ashwin suggested.

'No, I have to fly to Bangalore this evening,' The Lady said. 'I have an urgent meeting I can't miss. Hmm . . . I know! I'll send my driver across to pick you up. That way, you kids can get started right away.'

Ashwin knew that this was so far beyond the restrictions of his Mom Border that he shouldn't even be considering it. Mrs Kamath would eat him alive if he got into a stranger's car on the way to a stranger's house. He was just about to tell The Lady he couldn't do it when he hesitated.

The Lady was possibly a big-time celebrity. If he helped her find Prince, it would be the A–Z Detective Agency's biggest case yet. All the attention was bound to bring him countless clients. The Lady would be so happy with them that she'd send some rich clients their way too. And with two weeks left for the school trip, Ashwin was getting *really* desperate. He needed the money as soon as possible.

Going against his better judgment, Ashwin found himself agreeing to The Lady's request and dictated his address. Zubeida looked on curiously. Once Ashwin had hung up the phone, he immediately sat to write a note to his mother explaining where they were going. Since he wasn't quite sure himself, however, the note displayed a worrying lack of details. Ashwin hoped his mother wouldn't be *too* angry. In fact, he was hoping to get home before she even realized that they had left the house. He then explained the agency's latest case to the djinni.

'She cares more about her dog than she does about her maid?' Zubeida's eyebrows rose in amazement. 'Just when I thought humans couldn't get any weirder.'

'I wonder if she's a celebrity!' Ashwin gushed excitedly. 'She's being so secretive of her identity, and her voice did sound really familiar.'

'You'll find out when we meet her,' Zubeida answered.

The car arrived in thirty minutes, complete with a uniformed driver and tinted windows so nobody could see who was sitting inside. Ashwin made sure he had his magnifying glass. Then he and Zubeida sidled in to the back seat and spotted a partition between the driver and the passenger compartment. The two stared at each other and began chattering about their glamorous new case as soon as the car started to move.

'We'll definitely be able to charge a fat fee.'

'She may be a miserly VIP.'

'We have to find the dog first.'

'Luckily, dogs love djinn.'

They were so busy talking that they didn't notice when the car started slowing down. It was only when the driver opened the door next to Ashwin that the two detectives realized that they had reached their destination. Ashwin began whispering excitedly about what kind of mansion they might be about to enter.

The instant the two of them stepped out of the car, they stared ahead of them, then looked at each other in confusion. The two detectives were facing the Museum of Unusual Objects, and standing at the front door was—Mrs Bose.

'What are you doing here?' Ashwin asked the older lady in surprise. 'Wait . . . what are *we* doing here?'

'So lovely to meet you again, Junior Detectives,' Mrs Bose smiled. 'Come in, come in, and I'll explain everything.'

The destinies of djinn are tied to the destinies of humans. Throughout history, the leaders governing both the species made sure that their conflicts never escalated to wars. They were afraid that if humans and djinn began considering each other as enemies or, worse, broke off all ties with each other altogether, both worlds and species would face adverse consequences.

'What's going on?' Ashwin asked as they followed Mrs Bose into the house.

'I thought we were looking for a missing dog,' Zubeida frowned. 'What about Prince?'

'Curiosity is a trait well-suited to detectives,' Mrs Bose smiled in reply. 'That's my friend you spoke to over the phone. She should be arriving any minute.'

Ashwin grabbed Zubeida's hand and muttered, 'We have a seriously strange client. She doesn't even want to have us over at her house!'

'You must excuse my friend's paranoia.' Mrs Bose's sharp ears had caught the comment. 'She finds it very difficult to trust people. You can't be too careful in this age of so-called Internet journalists. They'll do anything for a juicy story.'

'A missing *dog* is a juicy story?' Zubeida asked.

'Only if it's a celebrity's missing dog!' Ashwin said triumphantly.

Mrs Bose smiled as she adjusted her glasses, but didn't say anything. She led them through the two rooms of the museum and over to the locked third room at the back. She fumbled for the silk pouch that hung from the waist of her sari and withdrew a key.

'As a reward for helping out my friend,' Mrs Bose said, turning the key in the lock. 'I'm going to show you my most prized possessions. Come on!'

Ashwin and Zubeida shot each other incredulous glances as Mrs Bose pushed open the door and led them inside. The room was bathed in darkness. Mrs Bose headed to a spot on the wall along the door and switched on the lights. A dull glow lit the room as Ashwin and Zubeida blinked to adjust to the illumination.

'I use a special kind of light in here to make sure that my exhibits don't suffer any damage,' Mrs Bose explained. 'That's why the room has no windows either. The sun's UV light is terrible for ancient treasures. Don't you want to come inside and have a look?'

The two detectives began to walk around, their jaws dropping in astonishment. Like the exhibits in the two rooms open to the public, this room also contained glass cases with handwritten notes propped up outside, explaining their contents. Unlike the exhibits outside, however, the ones in the secret room would have astounded even the most cynical of observers.

'A dragon's claw?' Ashwin whistled. 'Is this for real?'

'A spirit hunter,' Zubeida pointed at the instrument in front of her. 'And it looks like it's in excellent working condition. How did you get this? They're extremely rare!'

'Oh, that one required months of hunting,' Mrs Bose replied. 'And dealing with some very unsavoury characters. The owner nearly didn't sell it to me, but he was more open to reason after months of persuasion and a suitably fatter bank account. I always get what I want in the end.'

'Wow,' Ashwin breathed. He couldn't believe all the things he was seeing. Even after being in such close quarters with a djinni for weeks, Ashwin hadn't thought about the existence of other kinds of magic in the world. 'I suppose anything is possible.'

'That's right,' Mrs Bose replied. 'Anything *is* possible. Take my latest treasure hunt, for example. It's involved such painstaking effort for such little results that I very nearly gave up on it. Which would have been a shame, considering how close I now am to my prize.'

Curious about all the fascinating things she was seeing, Zubeida began to chat enthusiastically with Mrs Bose about how the old lady had found them all. Meanwhile, Ashwin walked around the room in a daze, his mind reeling with questions. If djinn existed, surely all the other things and creatures thought to be mere stories did too. Why had he never thought of that before? He had been so caught up with his goal and how Zubeida fit into it that he had never even considered the larger implications of her existence.

'So stupid,' Ashwin admonished himself. 'I've really been so stupid. I never even bothered to talk to Oz, even after everything I discovered!'

As he walked to the back of the room, he saw a large wooden table with a pile of papers held down by an old metal figurine. Ashwin neared the table to take a closer look. The papers resembled the handwritten signs tacked to each exhibit. The first sheet of paper had a yellow sticky note protruding from the top, with the words 'To be added' scrawled on it in a tiny hand.

'The Book of Life—a magical book which brings the stories inside to life . . .' Ashwin read on the first page. He moved the figurine aside and began going through the other notes.

'Magic Beans . . . Philosopher's Stone . . . the Helm of Invisibility . . . the Flaming Sword . . . a Kalpavriksha seed . . .'

He froze. Written on the sign in front of him was a single, heart-stopping word.

Djinni

Realization dawned on Ashwin with sudden clarity. He whirled around and marched over to where Zubeida and Mrs Bose stood, deep in conversation.

'Come on!' he said, grabbing Zubeida's arm. 'We're getting out of here!'

'What?' Zubeida looked at him in bewilderment. 'Why? The Lady isn't here yet!'

'I just remembered,' Ashwin said with a cautious glance at Mrs Bose, 'I haven't left a note for Mom. She'll be worried when she finds the house empty. You know how hyper she gets. She'll probably call the *police* in a second.'

'But what about Prince?' Zubeida had no idea what was going on. 'And I thought you *did* leave a—'

'We'll find him tomorrow,' Ashwin interrupted as he pulled her urgently. 'Let's go!'

Mrs Bose wasn't fooled.

'Trust me, Ashwin. You have no reason to be worried,' Mrs Bose said. 'Today is about to be the happiest day of your life. Now that you've figured it all out.'

Ashwin looked at the older lady warily.

'Name your price,' Mrs Bose continued, addressing Ashwin. 'You can go on a thousand school trips. You can even buy a house for your mother. No more moving houses and schools every year. Isn't that why you find it difficult making friends? As you can see, I've done my homework.'

'What is she talking about, Ashwin?' Zubeida demanded.

Ashwin didn't answer. They heard the sound of a door clicking shut behind them. Ashwin swung around to see a familiar figure standing inside the room.

'What are *you* doing here?' he demanded.

'He's here for me, of course,' Mrs Bose replied. 'He's already been such a great help. Surely you recognize him?' she asked Zubeida kindly.

'He's that friendly security guard,' Zubeida said slowly. 'I don't understand what's happening.'

The shaman shot her a look of pure malice. He reached into his pocket and his hand emerged with an iron chain.

'You will, dear, soon enough,' Mrs Bose assured the djinni. She turned to face Ashwin.

'How much will you sell it for?' she asked him. She noticed his expression. 'Oh, you don't have to worry about it. It will be very well taken care of, provided with everything it needs. A live exhibit after all these years? It'll be fascinating!'

'What?' the shaman snarled, twisting the iron chain around his clenched wrists. 'I thought I told you. The creature, like all its ilk, is wicked. You cannot trust anything it says or does.'

'It is no concern of yours what I do after I acquire it,' Mrs Bose replied calmly.

'But you promised me I could kill it!' the shaman argued.

As soon as Ashwin heard the word 'kill', his horrified brain unfroze.

'They're talking about you!' he yelled at Zubeida. 'Mrs Bose wants to buy you from me! She's the one who posed as Prince's owner! That man wants to kill you!'

'There will be no killing here.' Mrs Bose shot the shaman a quelling look. 'As for buying the djinni, I thought we had reached an understanding. I'll make you rich beyond your wildest dreams. And you can help me build my collection. All in exchange for the creature you possess.'

'You can't *buy* Zubeida!' Ashwin exclaimed. 'She's not a thing. She's not a creature. She's my friend!'

Zubeida looked at him in surprise.

'What a sickeningly sweet sentiment,' the shaman replied. 'An utterly foolish one, of course. Djinn don't have friends. They're creatures of evil and chaos. That's all they know.'

'I seem to have given you the impression that you have a choice,' Mrs Bose said pleasantly. 'Either you sell the djinni and earn some money. Or I capture the djinni anyway, without you earning a single rupee.'

'Zubeida!' Ashwin yelled suddenly. 'Remember the song!' He began singing the Bollywood version of the djinni's transformation spell.

Mrs Bose and the shaman looked at each other, baffled.

'Is this really an appropriate time for music?' Mrs Bose inquired. Ashwin ignored her and continued singing. Zubeida realized what Ashwin wanted her to do.

'I'm not leaving you here alone,' Zubeida said firmly.

'It's not me they want!' Ashwin said impatiently. 'Come back with help.'

The two adults had been trying to follow the seemingly absurd conversation, when Mrs Bose realized what was happening.

'Stop them!' she yelled at the shaman. 'They're trying to escape!'

Ashwin lunged at the shaman's stomach in a bid to distract them and tackled him to the ground. With the shaman squirming beneath him, Ashwin managed to kick the door open. Zubeida vanished and a housefly hovered over the spot where she had been standing. The fly buzzed angrily and flew out through the unobstructed doorway.

The shaman grabbed the boy in an iron grip to make sure he couldn't run. Mrs Bose walked up to the two sprawled figures and looked down at them.

'You've just made a huge mistake,' she informed Ashwin in a chillingly pleasant tone.

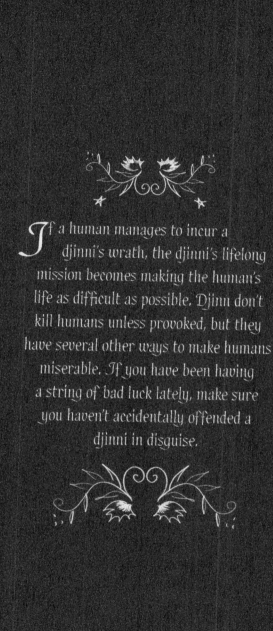

If a human manages to incur a
djinni's wrath, the djinni's lifelong
mission becomes making the human's
life as difficult as possible. Djinn don't
kill humans unless provoked, but they
have several other ways to make humans
miserable. If you have been having
a string of bad luck lately, make sure
you haven't accidentally offended a
djinni in disguise.

'What do I do? What do I do?' Zubeida buzzed around the lane outside the Museum of Unusual Objects. She flapped her wings nervously as she considered her next step.

She could look for a police station and drag some policemen over. But what if Mrs Bose denied her story and the policemen thought Zubeida was playing a prank on them? She could inform Mrs Kamath but she didn't know where her office was. Waiting for her to get home might make it too late.

A month ago, Zubeida would never have imagined that a human could have affected her in such a way. But now she was terrified for Ashwin's sake. As much as the boy exasperated her, if anything happened to him, Zubeida would never be able to forgive herself.

'Oz!' she exclaimed. 'I can ask Oz for help!'

The problem was that she didn't know the way back to Ashwin's house. She hadn't paid attention to the path the driver had taken earlier that afternoon. The last two

times she had been to the museum were with Ashwin and his mother.

She dismissed the idea of sending him a fire message. She doubted Oz would light a fire or even hang around too close to one in the heat of the Mumbai sun.

She tried to remember the path the train had taken the first time she visited the museum.

'This is impossible!' she thought, panicked. 'Ashwin's relying on my memory and I can never remember anything!'

She looked down at the lane below her and spotted a black-and-yellow taxi. They had taken a taxi from the railway station. She could ask someone where the nearest station was. She took a deep breath, tried to concentrate on turning back into a ten-year-old girl and began to sing.

After she got directions from a taxi driver, she ran to the station and looked at the names of all the stops to see which one jogged her memory. Her brain snatched fragments of a conversation with Ashwin about the odd station name featuring an elephant in the middle of the street.

Elphinstone Road

'Elphinstone Road!' she exclaimed. 'That's it!'

She ducked behind a wall, sang herself into a housefly once more and boarded the next train. From Elphinstone

Road station to Ashwin's housing society, she managed to get lost five times. But by alternating between her human and housefly form, Zubeida was able to retrace her path.

She flew in the direction where Oz usually sat and hovered over his sleeping form.

'OZ!' she yelled. 'WAKE UP! YOU HAVE TO HELP!'

Oz opened his eyes with a jerk and looked around for the source of the screaming. He spotted the fly, now suspended near his ear.

'Can't a person enjoy a nap without being harassed awake?' he demanded, sounding thoroughly disgruntled at the interruption. 'What's with the fancy dress, anyway?'

Zubeida rushed to explain everything that had happened.

'Come on!' she urged as she finished her story. 'We have to do something!'

'Do something?' Oz raised his eyebrow. 'Certainly you have to do something. Why didn't you inform the police in the first place?'

'Because you're better than the police!' Zubeida cried. 'Let's go!'

Infuriatingly, the older djinn made no move to obey her. 'I'm no longer an active participant in human or djinn affairs,' he said calmly. 'There's nothing I can do.'

'I can't believe you won't help!' Zubeida cried, outraged. 'Ashwin is in danger!'

'I did help,' Oz replied. 'I told you to go and inform somebody. Somebody who is not me. And you will have to hurry. Time is ticking.'

Zubeida glared at him. 'I don't want to be a castaway any more!' she yelled at him.

'That's some unexpectedly timed news,' Oz said, surprised by the change of subject. 'But good news nonetheless.'

'Because I didn't know that being a castaway turned a djinni's heart into stone!' Zubeida continued coldly.

Before Oz could reply, there was a loud pop and a sudden explosion of colourful smoke. The air was filled with the sounds of two djinn coughing. As the smoke cleared, Zubeida saw the shaman approaching them. He seemed to have resorted to a smoke bomb as a mode of distraction. He was dressed oddly, with several bands of metal wound around his forehead, arms, waist and legs.

'I knew you would come here,' he spat at Zubeida. 'To your own filthy kind.'

'Who are you?' Oz asked him, too puzzled to be insulted. 'And what on earth are you wearing?'

'Iron,' the shaman grinned.

Oz's eyes clouded over. Zubeida gasped. She moved away from where Oz lay and flew to the far side of the wall.

'You understand the position you are in, I see.' The shaman continued walking towards Zubeida. 'I've spent the last few days preparing for this encounter with you. That one over there took me by surprise. But there's no escaping me now.'

He reached into the bag that hung on his side and retrieved a spray can.

'Mrs Bose may want a live specimen for her museum,' he said, 'but I'm going to make sure the specimens are dead on arrival. That way, I'll still get paid, and I will also have rid the world of two of its foulest creatures.'

He shook the can and sprayed it at Zubeida. She instantly dropped to the ground with a thud. Shocked, she found that she somehow wore her human form instead of the garb of the housefly. Angry red rashes erupted all over her skin. When she tried to get up, a wave of dizziness left her incapacitated.

'What . . . what did you do to me?' Zubeida wheezed nauseously, trying not to throw up.

The shaman smiled at her weakened state in amusement. 'Liquid spray with concentrated iron,' he informed her. 'You didn't think I would meet you unprepared, did you?'

The shaman shook the can again as he broke into a brisk pace towards the other djinni.

'In all the books I've ever read, the problem with aspiring villains is the same,' Oz announced suddenly.

'And what's that?' the shaman asked, refusing to get distracted. He was five steps away from Oz . . . now four . . . now three.

'They all talk too much,' Oz replied with a lazy flick of his arm.

Where the shaman had stood a second before, there was now a gulmohar tree ablaze with scarlet flowers.

'If I'm ever going to take over the world,' Oz mused, 'I must remember not to give my enemies a long speech about my evil plans.'

'You . . . you turned him into a tree,' Zubeida said,

awestruck. 'I thought djinn could only perform illusions, not true magic.'

'The stronger the djinn, the stronger the illusion,' Oz replied. 'And that's another reason why you shouldn't become a castaway. The powers of djinn diminish the longer they're away from Djinnestan. At my peak, I could have turned this nincompoop into a mountain range. I had to settle for a tree.'

Zubeida shook her head at the thought of a mountain range in the middle of Mumbai. 'How long will this last?' she finally asked.

'The strongest illusion not only convinces the audience, but also the victim,' Oz replied. 'He'll remain a tree and, more importantly, *believe* he is a tree, until I return to Djinnestan.'

'So . . . forever?' Zubeida asked in hushed tones.

'Forever.' Oz nodded in satisfaction. He tried to stand up but had to thrust out his hand against the wall behind him for support, as he felt a spell of dizziness come over him.

'Ah,' he said. 'My powers have been stretched to their limits. No matter.'

He walked over to where Zubeida was trying to shake off the after-effects of the iron. Her skin was still covered in rashes and she felt a massive headache coming on. Oz bent down to help her up.

'Come on,' he said. 'We have some revenge to take care of.'

'Revenge?' Zubeida asked hopefully.

'Of course,' Oz replied. 'How dare some crackpot old human assume I'm a collector's item? Let's go.'

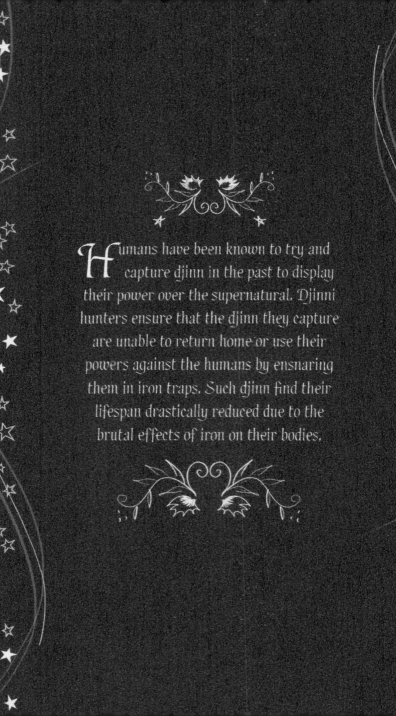

Humans have been known to try and
capture djinn in the past to display
their power over the supernatural. Djinni
hunters ensure that the djinn they capture
are unable to return home or use their
powers against the humans by ensnaring
them in iron traps. Such djinn find their
lifespan drastically reduced due to the
brutal effects of iron on their bodies.

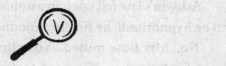

'There really is no use trying to bang the door down,' Mrs Bose informed Ashwin. 'The room is escape-proof. I had to make sure that nobody could get in, so you can be sure that you can't get out.'

The ten-year-old detective was locked inside the secret room of the museum and had periodically been banging on the door to get his captor's attention. Mrs Bose stood guard outside, waiting for the shaman to return.

'What are you going to do with me?' Ashwin's muffled voice demanded. 'My mother's going to notice I'm missing. And she'll definitely call the police!'

'Little boys in the city go missing all the time,' Mrs Bose replied calmly. 'And I've made sure that nothing leads back to me. The phone I used to call you was from an untraceable number. The police aren't going to solve this case.'

'Lots of people have seen me enter your house,' Ashwin pointed out. 'How do you think you can get away with this?'

'Oh, I have the shaman to take care of that,' Mrs Bose said. 'He'll hypnotize any inconvenient witnesses to make sure they don't remember anything.'

Ashwin's jaw fell open in astonishment. 'I'm not going to be hypnotized!' he finally announced.

'No,' Mrs Bose mused. 'Your involvement in this has been far too great. We need to find a more permanent solution for you.'

Ashwin certainly didn't like the sound of that. He hoped Zubeida was having better luck with her rescue operation, wherever she was.

'I do know someone who likes buying children and their freedom,' Mrs Bose said, sounding as pleasant as if she were discussing a shopping expedition. 'Maybe he'll be interested in a nosy, no-good detective.'

'No good!' Ashwin exclaimed, outraged. 'I'll have you know that we've solved plenty of cases!'

'Not so difficult when you had a djinni by your side, was it?' Mrs Bose dismissed his response. 'And in case you've pinned your hopes on her, know that the shaman is out on a djinni hunt. And he's not coming back empty-handed.'

'Actually,' a new voice announced, 'I doubt he's coming back at all.'

Mrs Bose turned around to find an old, shabbily dressed man standing beside the runaway djinni. Both of them looked the worse for wear but stood with a determined gleam in their eyes.

'So I think you should let the boy go,' the man suggested.

'Oz!' Ashwin's voice called out from behind the locked door. 'Is that you? Is Zubeida with you?'

Zubeida made for the door but Oz thrust out his arm to stop her. He wasn't sure what the lady had planned yet, and he didn't want Zubeida to take any unnecessary risks. Zubeida settled for calling out her reply.

'I'm here, Ashwin!' she yelled. 'We'll get you out!'

Meanwhile, Mrs Bose stood staring at the two in rapt fascination. The shaman had told her about his discovery of a second djinni, though they had eventually decided that the younger one would be easier to capture. But here they both were, walking into her house on their own. She really was the luckiest collector in the world.

'Where's the shaman?' she asked the two djinn.

'Currently playing home to a flock of birds, I suppose,' Oz replied. 'I turned him into a tree.'

'A tree,' Mrs Bose said softly, her mind whirring. This was clearly a powerful djinni. She could almost picture the pair as the newest live exhibits in her museum. Perhaps she could consider throwing open the secret door to fellow supernatural enthusiasts.

'He told me about your plan to turn djinn into displays,' Oz said, as if reading her mind. 'And I came here just to tell you exactly what I think of that.'

'You can't have been thrilled, I suspect,' Mrs Bose replied distractedly. What had she read about powerful bursts of djinn magic? Didn't the creatures need rest periods to attempt anything of consequence again?

'That would be putting it mildly.' Oz's calm tone matched Mrs Bose's. 'Unless you want to be turned into another tree to keep your friend company, I suggest letting Ashwin go.'

'And what if you still turn me into a tree after I let him go?' asked Mrs Bose, humouring the djinni.

'You have my word,' Oz responded.

'A djinni's word!' Mrs Bose laughed. 'As worthless as that shaman is to me now.'

'Perhaps I could turn you into a piece of furniture.' Oz looked at the older lady from top to bottom. 'Yes, I think you'd make for an excellent antique bookshelf.'

'If you could, you already would have.' Mrs Bose had grown bored of the charade. 'However, unlike you, I'm a doer, not a talker. And I'm not letting another djinni escape.'

She reached for the waist of her sari and withdrew a glinting net of finely woven iron wire. She unfurled it and threw it over the two djinn.

Oz's reflexes were sluggish after his recent bout of powerful magic, and he couldn't flick the net away to prevent it from ensnaring him. In the five seconds it took to reach him, however, he did manage to push Zubeida out of its way to safety.

Panicked, Zubeida couldn't remember the song to turn herself invisible. But as she saw Oz crumple to the ground and Mrs Bose advancing, she remembered the tune Ashwin had taught her.

As Mrs Bose came nearer, Zubeida sang the spell and vanished in a flash. Mrs Bose blinked, then walked over to a bookshelf and hit a button at the back. An alarm rang throughout the house and all the doors and windows slammed shut.

'The house is on lockdown,' Mrs Bose announced to the room at large. 'You might be invisible, little djinni, but you still can't walk through walls. You're going to be a part of my museum, whether you like it or not.'

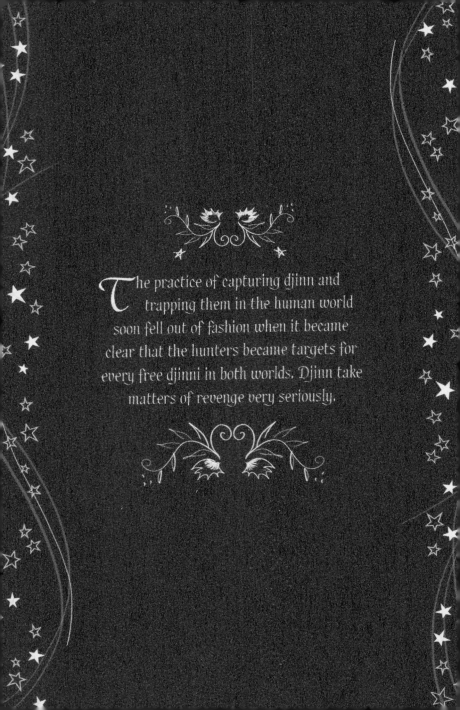

The practice of capturing djinn and trapping them in the human world soon fell out of fashion when it became clear that the hunters became targets for every free djinni in both worlds. Djinn take matters of revenge very seriously.

'What's happening?' Ashwin demanded, banging on the door. 'Where is everyone? What did you do?'

Mrs Bose dragged the nearly unconscious Oz over to the locked door. The prolonged contact with the iron net had interfered with the djinni's life force, and he found himself too weak to even put up a struggle. His skin had erupted in the same rashes that covered Zubeida's body. Mrs Bose secured the iron net around him to make sure he was completely trapped.

The invisible Zubeida watched the old lady retrieve a spray can similar to the one the shaman had used to incapacitate her earlier. Mrs Bose then dragged a chair, propped it against the curtained door and put her feet up on the iron-wrapped bundle in front of her.

'Stop that infernal racket,' she said in response to Ashwin's banging. 'The rescue attempt failed, that's what's happening. The one you call Oz is presently under my feet, and the one you call Zubeida is currently invisible.'

Hope leapt into Ashwin's chest. If Zubeida was still free, they had a chance after all.

Zubeida wasn't feeling quite as optimistic. If she tried to free Oz, the iron net would counter her invisibility spell and weaken her into revealing herself. Mrs Bose could then easily use the iron spray to capture her as well. And she had blocked the only way to reach Ashwin. Mrs Bose had told them herself—there were no windows into that room.

'What should I do? What should I do?' she asked herself. She couldn't think of a plan.

'The notebook!' she suddenly remembered. She could use the telekinesis spell to move the net off Oz without having to touch it. She would have to make sure to chant it correctly this time so she didn't accidentally set the older djinni on fire.

She reached into her back pocket only to find it empty. Her hand froze in dismay. *Where was the book?* Zubeida racked her brains, then hit her forehead in frustration. The notebook was currently under Ashwin's sofa back home where she had slid it for safekeeping after their most recent song-and-spell practice session. She would just have to go back and get it. She had no—

'This iron-particle-infused liquid is quite the invention,' Mrs Bose said conversationally, interrupting her thoughts. Zubeida pricked up her ears. 'The shaman was a genius. It's a shame where he ended up. Luckily for me, he made several litres of the stuff before he went and got himself turned into a tree.'

Oz grunted.

'What are you even talking about?' asked Ashwin. He had already grown convinced that the lady had been tottering on the brink of insanity, and had now finally cracked.

Several litres of iron water? Zubeida thought. *What good will that do?*

'In fact, even as we speak,' Mrs Bose continued, 'my electrician is busy cobbling together a way to adjust the house's central air-conditioning system. Any moment now, the AC should begin blowing iron particles into the air.'

Zubeida's breath caught in her throat. Her chest felt tight with dread.

'The invisible djinni should be revealed soon enough.'

Ashwin didn't quite understand what was going on. But he recognized a threat when he heard it. He decided to return Mrs Bose's threat with one of his own.

'If you harm my friends,' Ashwin growled, trying to sound as aggressive as he could, 'I'm going to destroy all your precious items in here.'

'The glass protecting all the exhibits is bulletproof,' she scoffed.

'Maybe,' came the reply. 'But is it ten-year-old-boy-proof?'

Mrs Bose paused. She had miscalculated. Locking a desperate child with her most valuable possessions hadn't been the wisest of decisions. She was sure the glass would hold up against Ashwin's assaults, but you could never tell how creative a desperate boy bent on destruction could get.

Zubeida didn't wait to hear the rest of the conversation. In a panic, she ran out of the room and turned into a housefly. She flew around all the rooms, looking for the smallest of gaps between windows and doors. But, just as Mrs Bose had said, there was no way out of the house.

She spotted some of the people who worked for Mrs Bose milling around in the kitchen, discussing the procedure to be followed during a lockdown.

'It must be a drill,' she overheard the cook talking to one of the maids. 'We'll wait in here until someone comes to fetch us.'

Zubeida briefly considered asking one of the domestic attendants for help. But she wasn't sure she could trust them. She decided to fly to the rooms on the two upper floors to see whether there was any way out through the roof.

She spent nearly fifteen minutes looking for a getaway route. But the house was securely locked down. Exhausted,

Zubeida fluttered down to a bed in one of the rooms. She was more afraid than she had ever been in her life.

Once the iron particles hit the air, she would be too weak to hold any form other than her human one, let alone try to run. Mrs Bose would easily be able to capture her. She couldn't escape, she couldn't rescue Oz, she couldn't rescue Ashwin. Zubeida was all out of options.

She transformed into her human form and desperately began emptying her pockets. She was looking for something, anything, that she could use to get out of this mess. But all she found in her front pockets were a small piece of mouldy cake, a broken rubber band and a ball of lint.

She rummaged around in the back pockets of her shorts. After a few seconds of fruitless hunting, she discovered a crumpled piece of rectangular paper.

'Where did this come from?' she muttered to herself.

She carefully unfolded the paper.

THE INDIAN JOURNAL

MAYA MENTA
CORRESPONDENT

TIJ: YOUR DAILY DOSE OF CURRENT AFFAIRS AND CULTURE

Parinita Shetty

The business card belonged to the journalist who was going to write about the A–Z Detective Agency. On the other side of the card were her email ID and phone number.

Zubeida looked around the bedroom in search of a familiar object. When she spotted the telephone, her eyes lit up.

222

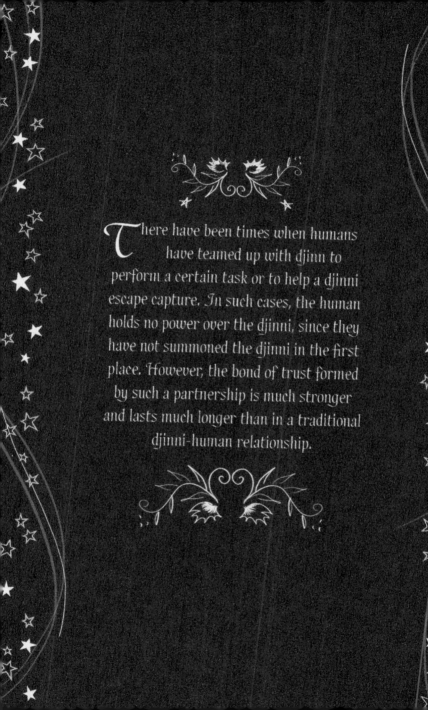

There have been times when humans have teamed up with djinn to perform a certain task or to help a djinni escape capture. In such cases, the human holds no power over the djinni, since they have not summoned the djinni in the first place. However, the bond of trust formed by such a partnership is much stronger and lasts much longer than in a traditional djinni-human relationship.

'I don't understand why it's taking so long,' Mrs Bose said coldly. 'You started working on it several hours ago.'

The electrician, a tiny man with a large moustache, refused to be cowed by her tone.

'It's a special order, madam,' he replied. 'I had to invent my own method by trial and error. I've never had to replace the coolant inside an AC before. Nobody else would have done such a professional-quality job for you. I had to first take apart the central—'

'All right, all right,' Mrs Bose said impatiently. She had no interest in listening to the technical intricacies. 'Just tell me how much longer.'

'It's nearly done,' the electrician said. 'All I have to do is connect two wires and turn on the AC using the main switches.'

'So why aren't you doing that, then?' Mrs Bose demanded. 'Why are you here chattering away to me like a baboon?'

'I just wanted to make sure this is what you want to do,' the electrician said, miffed. 'It'll ruin the system completely. You'll have to replace the whole thing. It will be very expensive.'

'Oh, who cares, you fool?' Mrs Bose cried. 'I can afford to replace the whole house, brick by brick, if I wanted to. Just do what you were told!'

The electrician shrugged. It was true what they said about these rich folk. Completely nuts, the lot of them. If she wanted to ruin her perfectly functional air-conditioning system, why should he care? He marched out of the room with as dignified an air as he could muster.

'Buffoon.' Mrs Bose rolled her eyes at his retreating back. 'Telling me what I can and can't—'

There was a sudden loud thud. It sounded like the front door being slammed open. *But that's impossible*, thought the two, alarmed. The whole house would continue to remain on lockdown mode until she keyed in the password to disable the alarm.

Just as she was wondering whether she should go and check what the noise had been, a troop of uniformed men and women burst into the room. Some of the larger figures banged against the exhibits of unusual objects and knocked a few to the ground.

'What—' Mrs Bose spluttered. 'What is the meaning of this?'

But she didn't feel as confident as she had just moments ago once she spotted the khaki clothes. How had the police entered her house?

'We'll be asking the questions,' one of the policemen barked. 'Put your hands where we can see them!'

'You cannot treat me like a common criminal in my own house,' Mrs Bose said authoritatively. 'Do you know who I am?'

'Quite an uncommon criminal, by the looks of things,' said a young woman who had followed the police, unnoticed. 'I've never seen such a well-dressed crook before. Is that an authentic Kantha silk sari you're wearing? My mother would kill for it.'

Mrs Bose was mystified at the appearance of the intruder. 'Who are you? Who gave you the permission to enter my house?'

'Oh, my name's Maya,' Maya introduced herself. 'I'm a writer for the *Indian Journal*. And being a police informant comes with a few perks. Entry into previously exclusive spaces, for example.'

Mrs Bose's blood ran cold. First the police, now a journalist? She had to get to the electrician and tell him to postpone the project. Once she got everyone out of the house, she could go back to djinni hunting in peace.

Suddenly, a ponytailed head popped out from behind the door at the other end of the room. A small figure with a tear-stained face ran inside, right up to Maya, and buried her face in her hands.

'You're here!' Zubeida sobbed. 'I thought we were never going to get out of here!'

Mrs Bose's heart sank at the sight of the djinni. 'Who is this girl?' she demanded. 'Why has everyone decided to break and enter into my house tonight?'

Zubeida looked at her in astonishment. Mrs Bose was quick to notice that behind the fake tears, the djinni's eyes glinted with mischief.

'Are you going to pretend you don't know me?' Zubeida asked, flabbergasted. 'After all you've done?'

'I have no idea what you're talking about,' Mrs Bose remarked, her razor-sharp brain trying to come up with a plan. 'Can someone please tell me what's going on?'

Zubeida looked up at Maya. 'She's the lady who kidnapped Ashwin and me,' she said in bewilderment. 'She threatened to do all sorts of horrible things to us. And now she's behaving like she's never even met me.'

One of the policewomen was trying to slip handcuffs around Mrs Bose's hands, but she was finding it difficult as the older lady kept swatting her away.

'Can you tell us everything that happened, beta?' one of the senior police inspectors asked Zubeida kindly.

Her voice quavering, Zubeida told the onlookers how Mrs Bose had befriended Ashwin and her using the pretext of their detective agency. Earlier that day, she had waited for them outside Ashwin's housing society and tried to trick them into accompanying her to her house. When they had refused, there was a violent struggle as she forced the two children into her car.

Oz, the homeless man who lived in the street outside the society, had noticed the scuffle and tried to intervene. But Mrs Bose managed to knock him unconscious and shoved him into the car so that no witness was left behind. One of the new security guards in their society had helped her kidnap them. But Zubeida didn't know where he was now.

Mrs Bose's eyes grew narrower with each fictional detail Zubeida furnished her story with. At the end of it, the policewoman had to prevent her from lunging at the djinni.

'She's lying!' Mrs Bose shouted. 'She's not what she looks like! Be careful of her!'

Zubeida blinked up at the older lady innocently while Maya shot her a look of disgust mixed with pity. The journalist turned to the djinni and said, 'Don't worry, Zubeida. You're safe now.'

The police took Mrs Bose into custody and declared the entire house off limits while they investigated it. They freed a delighted-looking Ashwin who was most impressed with the story Zubeida had come up with.

The police wanted to have a long chat with Ashwin and Zubeida, and the two had several questions for them in return. But Maya convinced everyone that the two needed to return home. Questions could wait.

They were driven home in the police van, accompanied by Maya who wanted to make sure they reached home safely. Ashwin and Zubeida excitedly exchanged details of what the other had missed. Ashwin congratulated Zubeida on her quick thinking, while Zubeida  admitted that the Bollywood songs had saved their lives.

'Bollywood songs?' Maya asked, bewildered.

Ashwin shot the djinni a warning look. He turned to the journalist and wore a puzzled frown.

'But how did you guys get in?' he asked, changing the subject. 'Mrs Bose told us it was impossible for anyone to get in while the house was on lockdown mode.'

'The alarm companies are more inclined to listen to the police than they are to their clients,' Maya replied. 'All we needed to do was tell them they were potentially shielding a child trafficker, and they promptly gave us the password to override her command.'

Mrs Kamath was waiting anxiously at the front door. She'd felt a vague sense of unease the moment she entered an empty house but she'd tried to convince herself that Ashwin was hanging out in the society, or playing at Zubeida's house for once. As soon as she'd found Ashwin's note, her dread deepened. When Maya had called to tell her what was going on, Mrs Kamath nearly had a heart attack. In the time that she spent waiting impatiently for the children to return, she had paced the entire society five times, yelled at the society's chairman for hiring security guards without background checks, drunk several strong cups of coffee offered by her neighbour Madhur and finally resorted to waiting in her own house.

As soon as she spotted Ashwin, she enveloped him in a tight hug, then extended her arms and pulled in Zubeida, Maya and the nearest policeman too.

'Would you like me to call your aunt and uncle?' Maya asked Zubeida when they had finally extracted themselves from the long hug. 'Won't they be worried?'

Ashwin exchanged a look with the djinni. 'Thankfully not,' he said quickly. 'We were going to have a sleepover here tonight, so they wouldn't have guessed she was missing.'

The police promised to return the next day to chat with the kids. Mrs Kamath invited Maya inside and demanded the uncensored version of the tale. With Zubeida and

Ashwin's help, Maya narrated all the shenanigans the two kids had been up to.

'I can't even begin to tell you how grateful I am for your help, Maya,' Mrs Kamath said finally. 'You're our knight in blue jeans!'

'Don't worry about it,' Maya smiled. 'I can't believe that I actually became a part of one of their mysteries! When everyone finds out about everything that happened today, your agency is bound to have clients lining up at the door.'

'Be that as it may,' Mrs Kamath said firmly. 'We're going to turn them all away. The A–Z Detective Agency is officially and permanently closed for business.'

'What?' Zubeida gasped.

'Why?' Ashwin wailed.

'Because I'm not going to risk either of you being mixed up with such dangerous characters ever again,' Mrs Kamath replied. 'Mrs Bose seemed like such a harmless old lady . . . You just *cannot* trust strangers.'

'But, Mom!' Ashwin protested. 'We've had plenty of good cases too. You can't shut us down just because of one bad experience!'

'Watch me,' Mrs Kamath retorted.

And however much they tried that night, there was no changing her mind.

TEN-YEAR-OLD DETECTIVES FOIL KIDNAPPING PLOT

JOURNALIST HELPS RESCUE TWO KIDNAPPED CHILDREN

WEALTHY MUSEUM CURATOR NABBED FOR KIDNAPPING CHILDREN

'DON'T TRY THIS AT HOME!' COMMISSIONER OF POLICE WARNS MYSTERY-LOVING CHILDREN

DETECTIVES OF THE FUTURE HELP NAB KIDNAPPER

A DETECTIVE WORKSHOP FOR CHILDREN BY THE MUMBAI POLICE DEPARTMENT

POLICE PRAISE QUICK-WITTED CHILDREN WHO LED TO KIDNAPPER'S CAPTURE

CHILDREN SET UP DETECTIVE AGENCY, GET ENTANGLED IN THEIR OWN MYSTERY

JOURNALIST TURNS CHILDREN'S BOOK WRITER AFTER THWARTING KIDNAPPING PLOT

HOMELESS MAN BECOMES A HERO

Friendships between humans and
djinn, while rare, are not unheard
of. Some djinn become attached to human
beings and act like companion spirits.
Such a permanent relationship between
a human and a djinni differs vastly from
the temporary one between a human
and a summoned djinni. If a human does
manage to become friends with a djinni,
the friendship tends to last for the entirety
of the human's life.

Two mornings later, there was a long line of neighbours clamouring to speak to Ashwin and Zubeida. Maya had written an article about their adventures which her newspaper had proudly carried on its front page the previous day. The editors had delightedly capitalized on their own journalist's involvement in the case and highlighted the story on their website as well as every other social-media page where their newspaper had a following.

While the *Indian Journal* was a small newspaper, catering to a very specific set of people, the story Maya narrated captivated the minds of journalists in other organizations too. Pretty soon, the story had gone viral, with news websites, bloggers and random people on Facebook, all posting admiring updates.

Mrs Kamath called in sick to work and spent the day making endless cups of tea and coffee for her curious visitors. She was exhausted by the constant ringing of the door and telephone. She solved the problem by leaving the door open all day and keeping the phone off the hook.

Not only had the article described the duo's adventures, it had also highlighted Oz's role in the rescue attempt. The world couldn't get enough of the story—two children teaming up with a homeless man to fight evil in the form of a cold-hearted museum curator.

Stunned by all the attention her article was receiving, Maya hurriedly finished writing her piece about the A–Z Detective Agency. She even managed to get a small interview with an exceedingly surly Oz. She posted both articles on her newspaper's website.

The response was instantaneous. People were dazzled by the three characters involved in the story. Offers poured in to sponsor Ashwin's school trip. Other people wanted to set up the detective agency with everything the mystery solvers needed. There were even some people who silently dropped books on Oz's street when he wasn't looking.

After asking everyone involved for their permission, Maya had decided to write a children's book based on the A–Z Detective Agency's adventures. Ashwin could hardly believe that he was going to be a detective other children would be able to read about.

The next few days flew by in a blur. Ashwin suddenly had enough money to register for the trip. The police held a small ceremony to felicitate Oz (they had had to hastily arrange it outside Ashwin's housing society since Oz refused to go anywhere else). Ashwin and Zubeida were the guests of honour.

The Police Commissioner held a press conference, where he praised the duo's quick thinking and Oz's alertness. But he also remembered to warn the young detectives (and any other children who were likely to be inspired by their escapades) against trusting strangers implicitly. However, he did encourage the idea of constant vigilance and honing one's investigative skills right from childhood. To that effect, the local police department held a detective workshop for children with Ashwin and Zubeida's help.

Mrs Kamath was too embarrassed to admit to the Police Commissioner that their detective agency was now defunct, particularly when he gifted Ashwin and Zubeida a customized detective kit, complete with smartphones that had several security apps downloaded in case of emergencies. While everyone was busy trying to convince Oz to give a speech, she sidled up to her son and whispered, 'If you promise to solve mysteries only under adult supervision, the agency can be re-established.'

'Deal!' Ashwin grinned.

That Thursday night, Ashwin lay on his bed, staring at the ceiling. He was leaving for his trip in three days. He should have been excited about all the new people he was going to meet. But all he felt was a strange feeling in the pit of his stomach. There was an unwelcome sense of things coming to an end.

Earlier that day, Oz had announced that he was leaving.

'I don't want to deal with all this attention,' he had grumbled. 'This is why I stay out of human affairs. Once you grab their fancy, they don't leave you alone.'

'What about all your books?' Ashwin had asked.

'You can take your eyes off them,' Oz replied. 'I'm taking them with me.'

'Where are you going to go?' Zubeida wanted to know.

'Oh, here and there,' the older djinni had replied vaguely. 'I don't have a plan yet. I'll wander around for a bit. Perhaps go see those pyramids everyone's going on about.'

'I'll miss you!' Zubeida gave him a sudden hug.

'All right, all right.' Oz squirmed as he tried to push her away. 'I hope you've got all that castaway nonsense out of your head.'

'For now,' Zubeida said with a gleam in her eyes. 'I can't wait to go back and show my classmates Ashwin's way of learning spells.'

Ashwin and Zubeida had sat together and memorized Bollywood songs for two whole days. Zubeida was now working on finding spell-and-song matches.

'Wait here,' Ashwin told the two djinn as he ran back to his house.

Zubeida and Oz exchanged mystified looks. Ashwin returned panting and clutching a box. He handed the box to Oz.

'What's this?' the djinn demanded.

'It's a smartphone,' Ashwin explained. 'The police got Zubeida and me matching phones. She's not going to need hers in Djinnestan, so you can have it.'

'What am I supposed to do with this?' Oz asked.

'Use it to keep in touch!' Ashwin cried. 'If you wait for another day, I'll ask Mom to help you get a SIM card. And I'll give you Internet lessons! You'll love the Internet.'

'I doubt it,' Oz retorted.

'Millions of things to read,' Ashwin assured him. 'You haven't even discovered Wikipedia!'

Oz's impending departure had reminded Zubeida that it was time for her to say goodbye to the human world. She had been away from Djinnestan for five weeks, and much to her surprise, she discovered that she missed home.

'Are you ready?' Zubeida peeped into Ashwin's bedroom.

They had decided to wait until Mrs Kamath was asleep for Zubeida to perform her spell. Zubeida had bid farewell to Ashwin's mother and told her she was going back home the next day.

Ashwin nodded silently and stood up. Zubeida showed Ashwin her notebook so he could see the spell that would take her back. He helped her draw a circle in the middle of the floor and they divided the task of drawing the symbols between them. Ashwin wrote the words in the centre of the circle and on the washbasin mirror that had been uprooted from its place once again. When it was all ready, they stood back to admire their handiwork.

'Don't forget to practise the spell-songs,' Ashwin reminded her.

'Don't forget to smile when you meet someone new,' Zubeida reminded in return. 'You have a very sullen face. You won't make friends if you're frowning all the time.'

'If you ever need another Bollywood song lesson, you can use this.' Ashwin reached behind him and grabbed the book on top. He handed it to Zubeida, who read the title aloud.

'*Adventures among the Djinn.*' Zubeida looked at him, confused. 'How is this supposed to help?'

'Well, I was talking to Oz,' Ashwin replied nonchalantly. 'And he said that djinn don't need to be summoned to leave Djinnestan. If they have an object from the human world, it sort of acts like an airline ticket. Each object can be used for a twenty-four-hour visit.'

'You . . .' Zubeida looked at him. 'You want me to use this to return?'

'It's called A–Z Detective Agency for a reason,' Ashwin said. 'I don't know how else humans and djinn are supposed to stay in touch. I doubt phones work in Djinnestan.'

'But don't you need this book for all your djinn research?' Zubeida smiled.

'I'm writing my own guide.' Ashwin smiled back. 'After all, I have a real djinni to help me.'

'Maybe I'll start my own agency back home,' Zubeida mused. 'A Bollywood spell tuition class!'

Ashwin laughed. 'Next time, I'll give you one of my Famous Fives. Hopefully it'll inspire you to start a detective agency instead.'

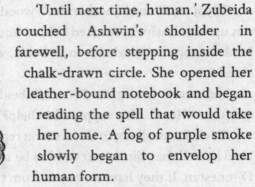

'Until next time, human.' Zubeida touched Ashwin's shoulder in farewell, before stepping inside the chalk-drawn circle. She opened her leather-bound notebook and began reading the spell that would take her home. A fog of purple smoke slowly began to envelop her human form.

Ashwin smiled at the now familiar sight. 'See you soon, djinni.'

Many humans believe that all djinn are creatures of chaos. While the red djinn do enjoy pandemonium, most djinn are merely creatures of habit. Djinn may spend a long time looking for a thing they enjoy——in rare cases, even their entire lives——but once they find something to love, they tend to devote most of their time to it.

Sunshine poured into the room through the large intricately carved window and through the circular stained-glass panels on the ceiling. The light illuminated the floor-to-ceiling bookshelves which encased the walls and the two closed doors on opposite ends of the room. Sconces lay scattered around the room filled with unlit candles.

The woman stood in front of the wooden table at the centre of the room. She adjusted her glasses before heaving open an enormous leather-bound tome.

'Where am I supposed to go next?' she muttered as she flipped through the pages. 'Come on, come on!'

She paused, as if she were waiting for the book to answer. In response, the pages began turning of their own accord. When they settled down, the woman leaned in to get a closer look.

'Mount Everest?' she read. 'At this time of the year? Why can't it ever be a nice town by the beach?'

It had been a few months since the woman had been chosen for her current position. When she had applied for a job at a library, this wasn't quite what she had expected. But she had soon thrown herself into the work and all the experiences that came with it. Most days, however, she couldn't help wondering who was in charge—the librarian or the library.

Once she finished reading the report, she pulled out a small, tattered diary from the pocket of her coat. It sported several rips and burn marks and looked like it had been dragged all over the world. The woman made a few notes, stuffed the diary back into her pocket and shut the leather-bound volume with a thunk.

She walked over to the bookshelves and reached for the giant globe which hung from the edge of a shelf. She idly spun it around a few times before pointing at the Himalayas. A muffled sound emerged from the closed door opposite the window. The crack under the door emitted a faint glow before fading back into darkness. This particular door worked with the globe to act as a gateway to any corner of the world.

'Remember, it's Mount Everest,' she warned the empty room. 'You're not allowed to send me to Timbuktu again just because you think it's funny.'

Over the months, the woman had discovered that the library not only had a personality of its own but a strange sense of humour to go with it. She grabbed her satchel from the chair and checked to see that she had everything she would need.

Suddenly, there was a knock on the door beside the window.

'Come back next week!' the woman called out. She didn't have time to deal with people at the moment.

The knock persisted.

'I'm busy!'

It increased to a pounding. The woman whirled around, marched over to the door and flung it open. On the other side stood a strange man with an untidy beard and even untidier clothes. He held a phone in one hand and a canvas bag in the other. He looked up at the woman, then back down at the Google Maps app on his phone and mumbled, 'Exit navigation.'

'Didn't I tell you to go away?' the woman asked in her most authoritative tone.

'They used to make you much politer back in the day,' the man barked. He walked inside the room uninvited and looked around.

'Not as big as the one I'm used to,' he grumbled, 'but I suppose it will have to do.'

'You can't be in there!' the woman squawked from the doorway. 'What are you doing here?'

'I'm here to offer my services,' the man replied. 'It's been a long time since I worked with a librarian. But I had forgotten how exhilarating the adventures could be. Where are you off to?'

'I'm going—it's none of your—wait, how do you know who I am?' the woman asked slowly.

'Well, this *is* one of the ancient libraries,' the man responded. 'And only librarians have access to the libraries. So I just made an educated guess. The library I used to work in was much more massive, of course. But I'll just have to get used to it.'

'Who *are* you?' the woman demanded.

'You can call me Oz.'

ACKNOWLEDGMENTS

The biggest, fattest thank you to Niyati, without whom this book would literally not exist. She's the one who had the idea for a book about a djinni, and she's the one who believed I was the perfect person to write it. I hope you approve of what my brain has come up with.

An equally enormous shout-out of gratitude to Nimmy and Purnima who made sure I actually sat down and wrote the story. Thanks for hunting down all the errors and making the book better (and for not sending me any Howlers whenever I was distracted).

Another big, fat thank you to Jit Chowdhury for making the book come alive with his illustrations. I can only sit back and sigh with a mixture of admiration and disbelief when I see my words so astonishingly captured.

I am also grateful to the quieter sections of the University of Glasgow library for offering absolutely no distractions and forcing me to work on the book.

My final hat tip goes to the TV show *The Librarians*. It is one of the best shows you've never heard of. It chronicles the adventures of a group of librarians who are constantly off saving mysterious, ancient artefacts and, occasionally, the world—which may or may not sound familiar.

Read More in Puffin

When Santa Went Missing
Parinita Shetty

'What do you mean I have to SAVE Christmas?'

All eleven-year-old Noel wants to do is live a normal life—something that's the tiniest bit difficult when your dad is Santa Claus. Just as Noel is struggling to cope with her dysfunctional family, her father goes missing in prime Santa Claus season!

When rumours of his disappearance start leaking, a reluctant Noel is packed off on a quest to prevent worldwide elfish panic. And if that wasn't enough, Gilmore, Coral and Bean, three elves with personality disorders, are along for the ride. This ragtag team has one week to visit six toy factories around the world and stop them from falling into chaos.

With crazy adventures at every turn and Santa still refusing to budge from the missing persons list, saving Christmas seems just a little out of their league.

Read More in Puffin

Gangamma's Gharial
Shalini Srinivasan

'There was a swish of a tail and for the first time in more than seventy years, the bazaar at Giripuram was Gangamma-less.'

At the ripe old age of seventy-nine and a quarter, Gangamma the gardener comes across a rather unusual object—a gharial-shaped earring that can take her anywhere in the world. On her very first trip, she tries to kidnap an apple tree, only to discover that it has a guardian—a sullen twelve-year-old girl—and an unlikely friendship springs up between the two.

But that's only the beginning of this story . . . or well, the middle, depending on how you look at it.

This book is no teleporter, but it *will* transport you (whether you re twelve or seventy-nine) to a fabulous (as in, fable-like) land of strange creatures and odd heroes, where things are never what they seem.

Read More in Puffin

Ayesha and the Firefish
Ajay Chowdhury

'Ayesha thought for a bit. Her parents had told her never to talk to strangers. But they hadn't mentioned anything about strange dolphins.'

Ten-year-old Ayesha has everything an adventurer needs—courage, cleverness, creativity and a complete lack of caution. But even Ayesha has to admit that the mission Shekina (the Queen of the Seas, no less) has charged her with may be slightly out of her league.

After all, it does involve saving the world. *Of course.*

And it's not like she has a fire-breathing dragon or a super-smart android as a sidekick. Try a snarky surfboarding snail instead.

Join Ayesha as she jumps headlong into an extra-extraordinary adventure that takes her halfway across the world (and a little beyond).

'A terrific fable about the planet's future and the power of children, written beautifully with an infectious charm and momentum'—AMIT CHAUDHURI

Muezza and Baby Jaan: Stories from the Quran
Anita Nair

'Would you like to hear a story, white camel?'

A camel with an appetite for stories and a clever cat who loves to snooze are lost in the unending desert. But they aren't your ordinary creatures and this isn't the story of just another chance meeting.

When these two wanderers, a djinn in the form of a baby camel and Prophet Muhammad's favourite cat, find each other amidst the lurking perils of the dunes, their dogged fight for survival fosters an unlikely friendship.

As Muezza the cat spins tales around the most enchanting nuggets of Islamic lore, such as the creation of Adam, the spite of Iblis the djinn-turned-angel, the gift of free will, the ninety-nine names of God, the mighty King Suleiman and much, much more, Baby Jaan can't help but be mesmerized. After all, who can turn down a good story?

Charmingly whimsical and breathtakingly illustrated, *Muezza and Baby Jaan* immerses us in an illuminating tale about a tender bond and, of course, some enthralling stories.